CW00376662

UNRAVELLING

Zoe's Submission -

One woman's journey to becoming a submissive

Book Two

Helena Sherwood

Introduction

Divorced and bored of the single life, of unfulfilling one-night stands, and sex that was mediocre at best, Zoe has met Adam through on-line dating. He is warm, funny, clever, generous, and the sex is amazing, but there's just one thing that Zoe is finding it hard to get to grips with.   Adam is a Dominant - and wants her to become his submissive.

After a few months of dating, she has fallen in love, and started to accept that maybe this new arrangement is exactly what she has been looking for. It isn't going to be an easy ride for either of them, as Zoe tries to maintain her independence, and Adam has to relinquish some of the control that he craves.

This isn't "50 Shades", but it is about real people, with real life problems, and real body hang-ups. It is about a woman whose decisions have always been ruled by her middle-class upbringing, and the desire to conform. When suddenly challenged by a man who wants her to give up her free will, her journey is bound to have a few bumps along the way.

Funny, sexy, sometimes difficult or awkward - I have tried to show that there's a whole world of kink out there, and we never really know what goes on inside other peoples' lives. We should never judge people by appearances. Instead learn to embrace whatever it is that makes you feel good, without the guilt or shame that society likes to impose. Above all, have fun!

Helena

I stood, looking into his eyes, and I knew I was where I belonged. I'd met Adam on an internet dating site just a few months ago, and he had taken me on a journey of discovery. He was a Dominant, and despite my initial reservations, he had asked me to become his submissive. I had resisted of course - even the word had such negative connotations for me. I was strong, independent, opinionated, and worked hard to pay my own way. After my divorce 3 years ago, I had vowed never to rely on a man for anything ever again, and that the only way I would enter another relationship would be on my own terms. Yet here I was looking into the face of the man who wanted to dominate me, but who I had fallen head over heels I love with.

The sex had been amazing right from the start, and Adam said he had seen very quickly that I had submissive tendencies. I had taken some convincing, and my habit of overthinking everything hadn't helped. I had spent weeks trying to justify my own feelings and misgivings, talking myself out of, then into, the relationship I was now involved in.

Being with Adam had made me feel safe and secure, and loved more than I ever had before. He was kind, generous, funny, intelligent, and although not traditionally handsome, he had a crooked smile and a twinkle in his eyes that brought me to my knees.

Then there was the sex. Oh god, the sex! When he took control, it was amazing. He had made me realise what I had been missing in my previous relationships. He had seen right away how easily I was dominated, how quickly I was able to give control to him. It had taken me by surprise, allowing me to switch off and give myself over purely to sensation.

Just before Christmas, work had dragged him away for a couple of weeks, and I had realized that I really couldn't stand to not be with him. I hadn't been an easy decision, and we had yet to see how the practicalities would work, but my Christmas gift to Adam had been the gift of my submission, along with a leather bracelet which carried a message in morse code, confirming his role as my Master.

"If you're going to be my sub, then you need to go into this with your eyes open Zoe. I need you to know I don't just want to play nice, to date you and make love to you. When I'm with you I want to own you. I want to tie you to my bed and use your body, to push you … the stuff I want to do to you might scare you, but you need to know you will always be safe with me. I need you to know what you're signing up for."

"Then show me." My heart was hammering in my chest, but I wanted this. I wanted him to push me to my limits and beyond. "Please … Sir."

"I like the way that sounds" his lip curled into a half smile, but then he suddenly grew serious. "Take off your clothes." I did as he commanded, heat pooling between my thighs even as I removed the sequin embellished blouse and skinny black jeans that I had worn for our Christmas dinner. I threw them onto the sofa, then took off the black lace bra and pushed the matching knickers down my legs. Even now, the intensity of his gaze made me feel self-conscious again, and I moved my hands to cover myself. He glared at me, his disapproval obvious, so I dropped my hands to my sides, looking down to see the outline of his cock straining against the dark denim of his jeans. Adam's eyes travelled over my body, and my nipples tightened under his gaze. He reached out and cupped my breast, dragging his thumb over my sensitive nipple.

"So gorgeous" the deep desire in his voice made me melt, and I shuddered as he bent and sucked my nipple into his mouth. I threaded my hands into his hair, holding his head to my breast and urging him forward, needing more, but he stood, and backed away.

"Please Adam." Was he really going to drag this out and make me beg? "I'm sorry. Please Sir."

"Remember, I'm in charge of your pleasure. Do as you're told and trust me to give you what you need." My throat suddenly went dry, and I swallowed hard. I was aching to touch him, to undress him and feel his skin against mine, but I fought the urge to make a move until instructed to do so.

"Now, go upstairs and kneel at the foot of the bed, head bowed, hands on your thighs." His words caused a flood of arousal, and it took all the willpower I had not to run up the stairs two at a time. Adam's bedroom was furnished with rich deep colours and dark woods that suited his masculinity. I settled onto my knees and the foot of the bed, thankful for the thick pile of the carpet.

A few moments later Adam came into the room. He pulled closed the heavy lined curtains, then turned on one of the bedside lamps, casting a warm glow over the room.

"Where's your collar?" he referred to the necklace that he had given me just a couple of weeks before. It was a silver choker with a pendant which bore a triskelion symbol, significant within BDSM circles.

"It's in the drawer beside the bed. I'm sorry… I didn't know whether I should put it on or not."

He went over to the bedside and took the silver choker out of the black case, then returned and bent to fasten it around my throat. "From now on, I will expect you to be wearing this whenever you come here. You will keep it on whenever you are here, and at any other time when you are instructed by me to wear it. Now, stand up."

I got to my feet, and he trailed his fingers down my arm, his touch unbearably light, and causing goosebumps to rise on my skin. He moved his hand down over my hip, then it dipped between my legs, finding me already wet and wanting.

"So hot and ready for me." His mouth was against my neck now, and he pressed his thumb against my clit, causing a jolt of pleasure. I moaned, and grabbed him, my nails digging into his shoulders, as his thumb circled, while his fingers swirled over my wet folds and dipped inside my entrance. Jesus, how could I be so close already. I swear he could tip me over the edge in just a few more seconds.

"Don't even think about it" he chuckled. "I haven't given you permission to cum yet." He continued to stroke his fingers in and out, and I whimpered, my legs beginning to quiver until I thought they wouldn't take my weight for much longer.

Suddenly he pulled back, and I opened my mouth to protest but he silenced me with his fingers, coating my lips with my own wetness. Then he took my face in his hands and claimed my mouth with a fiery kiss, which sucked the breath from my body.

"You're going to have to learn to control yourself" he said as he pulled away again. "Now, tell me what you want, what you need." He knew how difficult I found it to talk about my desires, yet he found ways to force the words from me. I bit my lip, and with my head bowed slightly, I looked up at him from under my lashes.

"I want to please you, Sir." His eyes burned with desire, and he pulled the t-shirt he was wearing over his head, then placed a firm hand on my shoulder, pushing me downwards.

"On your knees." I sank down again on the plush carpet. Just a few months ago, I'd never imagined letting a guy command me like this, speak to me like his whore. I should have been appalled when he called me his slut, but something inside me made me ache to please him. He unbuttoned his jeans and pushed them down his thighs along with his boxers, freeing his erection. He stroked his cock, bringing it to my face. "Now, open that pretty mouth of yours and show me how much you want to please me."

He grabbed a fistful of my hair, pulling so tightly that it made my scalp tingle, and tilting my head back to the angle he wanted it. Then with a low groan he slid his cock into my mouth. I took it as deep as I could, closing my eyes as I savoured the slight salty taste of him. I ran my tongue along the underside of his smooth shaft, easing back to lick the swollen head. He pushed forward again, his fingers twisting in my hair, and I let out a stifled cry around him.

"Don't close your eyes, look up at me." I raised my gaze to his face, his eyes filled with such hunger, spurring me on to take him into my throat. "Oh god that's so good. Relax babe, take all of me. You look so beautiful sucking my cock."

I didn't know any fancy techniques for giving head – it wasn't something I'd especially enjoyed in the past, and I'd never had anyone really offer any encouragement. With Adam it was different. Just hearing that sharp intake of breath when I took him in my mouth, or the way he moaned when my tongue pressed against the underside of his cock, that was all the encouragement I needed. Soon he was hitting the back of my throat with each long steady stroke. I reached up and cup his balls in my hand, and he moaned, but then stepped back and pulled out of my mouth.

"I didn't say you could touch me."

I blinked, surprised by the sudden withdrawal. "I'm sorry, I just thought…"

"But you're not here to think. You're mine remember, and you need to listen, and to obey. That's all."

"Ok. I mean I'm sorry, Sir."

"Get on the bed. Face down." I got to my feet and climbed onto the bed with wobbly legs. "You still find it hard to give up control don't you." He moved over to the dressing table and opened one of the drawers. "So, I'm going to help you out, and take it from you." He took out the padded cuffs that he had used before, but this time, instead of clipping my wrists together so I could undo them myself if I needed to, he fastened each one in turn to the posts at either side of the headboard. Then he took a strip of black fabric and positioned it across my eyes, tying it tightly at the back of my head. Suddenly I began to panic, my heart was racing, and I yanked my arms in the restraints, my hands balled into tight fists.

"Shhh." His voice was instantly calming, and he stroked a hand against my back, as my breathing slowed. "You have your safe words remember?"

"Yes Sir." My voice was barely a whisper. He had given me safewords when we had spent a weekend at a hotel just a couple of weeks ago. A simple traffic light system, green for go if something felt good and I wanted more, yellow meant I wanted him to slow down or back off a little, and red would make him instantly stop what he was doing and release me.

A loud crack broke into my thoughts as he brought his hand down across my bum, causing fire to flare in the skin. I cried out, the sound muffled against the bedding. Then the sting was replaced by a warm pleasant heat and my pussy throbbed in response. I was still surprised by the way my body responded when Adam spanked me.

"Up on your knees." Adam gripped my hips and helped me to bring my knees up underneath me, so my face and chest were still pressed against the bed, the restraints at my wrists preventing me from lifting my upped body. "Fuck Zoe, you have no idea how sexy you look with your arse in the air and my handprint on your skin." Suddenly he brought his hand down on my opposite cheek, and I bit my lip, moaning with the combination of pleasure and pain. He spanked me again and again, and I writhed beneath him, crying out as he spanked every inch of my buttocks and the backs of my thighs, never hitting the same spot twice. My body was flooded with endorphins and my head began to swim, while moisture ran down my thighs, betraying my need.

"Fuck. Yellow!" I cried out, as the last blow landed against my pussy, causing me to lurch forward and away from his touch. The spanking was then replaced with the soft strokes of his hands against my heated skin, the gentle caresses soothing over the glowing flesh. He dragged his fingers up the backs of my thighs, and it felt like a surge of electricity when he touched that sweet spot at the juncture between my thighs and my bum cheeks. I lifted my head and moaned.

"Oh god, please." I parted my knees, opening myself up to him, not caring what kind of a slut that made me. "Please, I need you inside me." He moved his hand between my legs and dragged a finger up between my folds.

"Jesus, your fucking dripping!" I tried to push back against him, to take his finger deeper inside me. He pulled his hand away and I felt his weight shift on the mattress behind me. Then I felt his strong hands grasp my hips, lifting my backside and spreading my thighs to him.

"Is this what you want?" The head of his cock pressed against my opening. Again, I tried to press back, to force him into me, but the cuffs were too tight against my wrists and held me firmly in place.

"Tell me," he growled, leaning down to kiss my back and neck. "Tell me what you want me to do to you."

I was panting, aching with desire to the point of pain. "Fuck me. Please Sir, fuck me hard!"

With one sudden movement he buried himself inside me, causing me to cry out, suddenly filled so completely. He was still for a moment, leaning down and pressing his chest against my back. He wrapped his arm around my stomach, pulled out almost all the way, then thrust again hard. One hand was on my hip, while the other moved down over my neatly trimmed bush and his fingers dipped down to my swollen bud. He thrust into me with long smooth strokes, burying himself deep, over and over again, while his fingers constantly teased, intent on keeping me at the edge and holding me there until my moans became more pitiful and pleading.

"That's it, beg me for it. You want to cum?" His fingers began to pinch and tug, while he slammed into me from behind.

"Please, oh god yes." It felt like fire flooding through my veins and pouring into my pussy as he suddenly pinched my clit, rolling it between his fingers, and I screamed into the mattress. Every nerve exploded and sent me crashing over the edge in the all-encompassing wave of orgasm. Adam was still driving into me with frantic thrusts, his fingers bruising my hips as he pulled me against him, and my cunt rippled and clenched against his hardness. He cried out with his own release as my pussy continued to pulse and milk his cock, until finally he stilled his hips, pressed hard against my stinging backside, and I could feel him twitching inside me.

Adam bent and kissed my shoulder, and I collapsed against the bed, my legs giving way beneath me. He pulled off the blindfold and rolled off me so I could stretch out my legs, then he reached up and released each of cuffs that held my wrists. I lay still, breathing hard, still face down against the bed, too exhausted to speak. I winced as he stroked his hand down over my bum.

"Too much?" he whispered, kissing the back of my neck. "You could have stopped me any time. Why didn't you?"

"I'm fine, honestly I am." He stroked my cheek, pushing a strand of sweat-damp hair from my forehead, and I smiled up at him "You make me feel so...well, alive."

"I love seeing you like this" he said, planting a kiss on my nose. I frowned, well aware that I must look a complete mess. "I love it when you're flushed and sweaty and look like a woman well satisfied. I want to keep you in my bed and looking like this all the time."

"Well, you promised me a few days of mind-blowing kinky sex. I'm all yours."

"Good," he soothed. "Because you know I will never hurt you, Zoe. You're safe with me. I'll push you, but never further than I know you can go. Is this really what you want?"

"Yes, it is." I gulped, suddenly nervous. "I don't want you to go easy on me Adam. If I'm going to do this, I want all of it. All of you."

I pulled the duvet up, suddenly cold as the sweat evaporated from my body, and snuggled into the crook of his arm. "I need a nap" I yawned, "And then a snack. I'm starving."

He chuckled and pulled me closer. "Nap first, then I'll make us something. Close your eyes baby."

About forty minutes later, Adam woke me with a cup of tea. He was wearing his grey sweatpants and a t-shirt, and he smelled fresh and clean from the shower. "Come on, if you sleep too long now, you'll be awake all night."

"That doesn't sound like a bad thing" I winked at him, taking the mug of tea from his hand.

"Behave" he said with a smile. "Go and have a shower if you want. I'm going to put some supper together" and with that, he left the room. I had a quick shower and dressed in my favourite comfy yoga pants with a baggy sweatshirt.

We ate cheese and crackers and drank red wine, half watching the rubbish that passed as Christmas television. Adam had been working yesterday, Christmas Day, but had cooked us an amazing Christmas lunch today instead, so neither of us wanted anything more than a snack. I was picking at a bit of cheese, just playing with it really.

"What's on your mind, sexy?" He put his own plate down on the coffee table and took my hand.

"What's *not* on my mind." I replied. "I'm just nervous I suppose. Over-thinking again. I don't really know what I'm doing - what this involves, and how it's going to change our relationship. I mean, we were doing fine, dating and having the kinky sex, but I don't know how being your 'sub' is going to change that yet. I'm so afraid that I won't live up to your expectations. I've never done this stuff before – whatever this is."

"Come here" he said, patting his thigh. I hesitated, not least of all because at five feet eleven and a curvy size 16 I was no lightweight, but then remembered Adam's warning about following instructions without question or hesitation, so I scooted over and sat on his lap. One arm wrapped around my back, and the other settled on my thigh. He was six feet four, with broad shoulders, and just enough "padding", and I settled against his shoulder, enjoying the novelty of feeling small in his arms.

"Firstly, I don't much care for that word – kinky. Safe, sane and consensual, and if we both enjoy it, that's all the matters."

"I know, I get that, but won't we ever just make love? Does it always have to be a bit... freaky?"

"I'm sorry sweetheart, I just don't get off on all the soft stuff. I just always needed the extremes I suppose. I want to command you, and watch you lose yourself."

I sighed, not sure how to voice what I was feeling. "I spent years in a marriage where I was treated like property, called names, mentally abused. Why would I want to be treated like that again? Is there something wrong with me, that I get off on that?"

"Firstly, I'm not your ex-husband. He was an abusive dickhead by the sounds of it, who needed to make you feel small just so he could feel like a man. I adore everything about you, you're amazing and gorgeous, and clever, and … need I go on? The fact that you like a little rough sex where you can give up control doesn't make you wrong, or sick." He paused. "How much wine have you had?"

"Not much. I'm still on the first glass, why?"

He tapped a finger against my forehead as he spoke. "Because I need to stop you from overthinking for a while. Come on, I want to show you something." We got up and he took my hand, leading me out through the open plan kitchen/diner. He grabbed a bunch of keys from a hook on the wall as we passed the utility room and downstairs shower room, then he unlocked a door which led through to the garage. There were the usual tools on wall racks, although it was remarkably tidy and clean. Just inside the were floor to ceiling cupboards and shelves, and at the front of the space, behind the garage door was his bike – the BMW R1200GS that he'd told me he only rode in good weather these days, when the sun was melting the tarmac. In the middle of the space, a punchbag hung from a seriously heavy-duty hook in the ceiling, above a square of grey rubber matting.

"Do you trust me, Zoe?" he said. He didn't wait for me to answer, but instead turned and took the weight of the punch bag, lifting it down from the chain which fastened it to the ceiling hook. "Take your clothes off."

"What, here?" I looked around, wondering what he meant. "I'm not having sex in the bloody garage!"

"Don't make me ask twice." He frowned. "And I never mentioned sex."

I pulled the sweatshirt over my head and hung it on a hook on the wall, then did the same with my yoga pants. Adam glared at me, and I removed my underwear, his gaze causing me to feel all hot and bothered again.

"The way you blush all over is one of the sexiest things I've ever seen." He ran his thumb over my lower lip, and I opened my mouth, suddenly overwhelmed by the urge to suck or bite it. "Stand there, don't move." One of the keys unlocked the tall double doors of a cupboard, which was fitted out like a wardrobe. I could see a couple of helmets on the top shelf, and there were leathers and a lightweight waterproof bike jacket hanging on a rail, with 3 pairs of boots at the bottom. On another shelf was a Bluetooth speaker, and he scrolled through some music on his phone, before settling on a playlist of guitar heavy rock music with the thumping beat that he loved. Then he pulled out a leather holdall, which he dropped on the soft mat. He unzipped the bag and inside were coils of rope of assorted colours, all tied neatly in bundles. He took out a shank of red cotton rope and dropped it on the floor at my feet. Then he went to a drawer and took out black padded eye mask, like a sleep mask, and a knife with a curved blade of about five inches. He placed them both on the shelf close to where we were stood. Suddenly my body was covered in goose bumps, and my nipples stood out like bullets.

"I fucking love the way your body responds to this" he said, suddenly grabbing my hair, and pulling my head back to look up at him. "You get off on a little fear, don't you?" He watched me as I swallowed hard. "Now, time to cure you of your overthinking and get you out of your own head."

He moved me into position in the centre of the mat, immediately below the hook where the punchbag had been hanging. He placed the blindfold over my eyes, and I fought the rising panic.

"Sshhh. You're safe" he placed his lips against the racing pulse in my neck, cradling me in his arms until my heart rate slowed a little. "Now, if anything starts to go numb or tingle, or you start to panic, use your safe words. If you say Red, I'll stop immediately, and cut the ropes. OK?"

I nodded. "I know. Thank you."

He took my hands, positioning them with my palms together in front of me. I heard him untie the rope, shaking out the coils which thudded against the floor. Then he held a loop across my wrists, wrapping the doubled rope around, then began to weave it in and out of my fingers. The ropes were looped around my wrists, coming together in tight knots, then separating and winding around each of my arms with a series of loops and more knots. The two loose ends of the rope were draped over my shoulders. I heard the click of a carabiner in the loop of rope between my hands, then he raised them up over my head, and there was another click as he fastened them to the chain which hung from the ceiling.

My breaths were becoming more shallow, and I felt my skin warming, even though it was cool inside the garage. I had expected to feel claustrophobic and panicky, but instead my breathing slowed, and I felt suddenly calmer, all anxiety draining away, concentrating on the sound of Adam's breathing as he moved around me. He was stood in front of me now, and I could feel his breath just inches away from my face. He took more rope and holding it against my chest with one hand, he moved the other around my back, then swapped hands, to wrap it around my torso. The rope ran across my rib cage, just below my bust. Then he knotted it between my breasts, then the two ends wrapped around my upper chest, under my armpits and around to my back. There he crossed and knotted it again, bringing the ends up and over my shoulders. He moved around me, criss-crossing the rope around my chest and torso, down to my waist. It was tight enough that the knots pressed into my skin, but not so tight as to hamper my breathing.   His hands were steady and confident as he moved over my skin, and I became aware of his clean masculine scent as he moved around me. I sighed and allowed my head to fall forward, suddenly more relaxed than I'd felt in ages, enjoying the feeling of relinquishing all control once more.

As the rope held me tightly, I felt as if I was floating, my legs felt weak. I allowed the rope to take my weight, supporting my entire upper body as I leaned against Adam. My head was swimming, and as his hands skimmed over my body, over the rope bindings, I felt as if the whole world were just melting away – the only thing that mattered was me and him, here and now. I relaxed against him, feeling dizzy and lightheaded, almost euphoric, and hung there, losing all sense of time and place. "You look so fucking perfect right now" he kissed me softly, flicking his tongue into my mouth and wrapping his arms around me. I felt totally helpless, all movement restricted, yet lighter than air - better than any alcohol buzz. I closed my eyes, hearing nothing but the slow steady whooshing of my blood rushing in my ears, and feeling electricity from Adam's fingers against my skin. He stroked me softly, touching every inch of me, my neck, shoulders, my breasts which were lifted and separated by the rope, my back, my stomach, my thighs and buttocks. He wasn't touching me in a way that was overly sexual, and avoided both my nipples and my pussy, but it was nonetheless erotic. My thoughts began to slow like honey, and I felt a dreamlike buzz taking over my senses. I felt as if I wanted to dissolve into a tingling puddle, and drifted as if I were in a trance, for I don't know how long.

Sometime later, Adam removed the blindfold, and lifted me off my feet as if I weighed nothing, freeing my hands from the hook above my head. He placed me on my feet, holding me until I regained my balance, then began untying the rope bindings, freeing first my arms and hands, and massaging my neck and shoulders, then rubbing my arms to help get the circulation going and prevent any stiffness.

"How did that feel?" he asked, stroking my hair as I leaned against him.

"Amazing… I can't really describe it" I whispered. "It felt like I was floating."

 He smiled, brushing tears from my cheek that I didn't even know I'd shed. Then, once I was steady enough on my feet, he began to unlace the corset of rope that framed my breasts and hugged my ribcage. His fingers traced the dents and patterns on my skin made by the knots and the weave of the rope.

"I'm so proud of you" he kissed my shoulder. "And you looked amazing – next time I'll take some photos."

"Oh Adam, don't. Please" I instinctively covered myself and stepped forward to reach for my clothes.

I pulled the sweatshirt over my head, then looked up to see a combination of hurt and disappointment in his eyes.

"Why do you do that? You don't think I'd share the pictures with anyone, do you? I just wanted to be able to show you what I see – you're so beautiful, your body is amazing. You should be proud of it. But instead, you reject every compliment or put yourself down." He gripped me by the shoulders, forcing me to look up at him. "Why do you still not trust me?"

Suddenly tears were pricking at the back of my eyes. "I'm sorry, I just don't feel gorgeous. I'm overweight, and everything wobbles, and I've got stretch marks, and…"

"Stop." he cut me off. "Do you think that's what I see when I look at you? I see a beautiful, sexy woman. I see those incredible tits, with pretty, pink nipples that harden at the slightest touch, and that beautiful long neck where I can feel your pulse racing when you're excited for me. I see the hourglass curve of your waist, and the swell of your hips and that rounded arse which I just ache to spank it until it glows pink. And this…" his hand dipped between my legs, stroking my pussy lips. "Do you know what it does to me, knowing you get so hot and wet for me?" He withdrew his hand and raised it to his mouth, sucking my juices from his fingers, and making me blush all over again. He pulled me into his arms, and kissed me hard, his hands digging into the soft flesh of my bum and pulling me against him.

"Stop challenging me, Zoe. You know you won't win. I'll enjoy the battle, but you? Probably less so." With that he brought his hand down hard against my bottom, the smack against bare skin echoing in the empty space of the garage.

"Come on" he said, moving to switch off the stereo. "Time for bed." I took the rest of my clothes from the hook and followed him back through the kitchen. "Go on up, I'll grab us some water and load the dishwasher." He moved through the lounge, gathering up the plates and glasses, and I headed up the stairs.

I used the loo and brushed my teeth, then sat on the bed, thinking I really ought to have another shower, but suddenly feeling so exhausted that I really couldn't be bothered. I dropped my clothes onto the bench and climbed between the cool sheets. Adam came into the bedroom and placed a glass of water on the bedside table. I took a long gulp, then settle back against the pillows, and closed my eyes.

"Night sexy" said Adam, kissing me swiftly on the lips before laying down beside me. I smiled, enjoying the possessive gesture of his arm draped across my belly, and turned to my side so could spoon against my back.

The next morning was cold and grey, but the sun was trying hard to break through the clouds. I woke before Adam, so I went downstairs and made us a coffee, and brought it up to the bedroom. I got back into bed beside him and pressed myself close to his warm back. He rolled towards me, shifting position so I could snuggle into the crook of his arm.

"Morning hot stuff" he said sleepily, kissing me on the head.

"Morning" I smiled, my fingers stroking the sprinkling of chest hair. "I brought us coffee. I can fetch some toast too if you like?"

Adam shuffled upwards to a semi-sitting position and reached over for the coffee mug. "No thanks, no food in the bedroom. Sorry, it's a pet hate – crumbs in the bed."

"Ok. Good job I checked" I sat up and took a sip of my own coffee. "Any other rules I need to know about?"

"Mmm, maybe we'd better start with you wearing my collar. You need to put it on before you arrive, and keep it on all weekend, unless I tell you to remove it."

"Why would you want me to remove it? You mean as a punishment?"

"No. I couldn't punish you if you weren't wearing it, could I? You'd no longer be my sub, so I'd have no right to punish you." I looked puzzled, but having put down his coffee, he leaned close to me. He placed one hand around my neck, his thumb resting against my throat. "But I might decide to replace it with something a little more sturdy from time to time; perhaps more restrictive." My eyes widened and I swallowed hard, but he withdrew his hand and chuckled. "Oh, this is going to be so much fun babe." With that, he threw back the covers and got out of bed, heading for the bathroom, although he wasn't quick enough to hide the raging hard-on.

"You want a hand with that?" I asked, looking pointedly at his rigid cock, then smiling up at him, with my best wide-eyed innocent look.

"Not this time babe, but hold that thought for later." He turned on the shower. "We've got stuff to do today." I waited for him to finish in the bathroom, then showered while he got dressed. When I came back into the bedroom, Adam was dressed in his jeans and the new sweater I'd got him for Christmas, and was looking out of the bedroom window.

"It's trying to brighten up, I think. I need some fresh air, so we can go for a wander in a bit and get lunch while we're out."

We enjoyed a leisurely breakfast, then I decided to write in the journal that Adam had given me for Christmas while he answered a couple of work emails. I wrote about being tied up in the garage the night before and tried to put into words how it had made me feel, but I found it impossible to describe the emotion that I had felt, so gave up. I chuckled to myself, suddenly aware that I was over thinking again. It was a bad habit I'd had since being a teenager, and I knew it wasn't something I could just stop doing, no matter how much I wanted too.

Later that morning we set off towards the estate with the garden centre that I knew well. It had a lake and a park that we could walk around, plenty of shops and stalls to browse, and a couple of half decent restaurants where we'd be able to get a late lunch. The car park was busy, and there were lots of people milling around, all out to walk off the glut of Christmas food and get some fresh air after a couple of days in front of the television. We walked around the lake but there was a bitterly cold wind blowing across the water, so I was glad when we got back around to the shopping village.

"I think we need a coffee too warm up" said Adam, as I pulled my scarf tighter around my neck.

"We can do better than that – there's a stall down at the end that does the most amazing hot chocolate. It's right by the shop where I had your Christmas gift made. The owner, Kate is a submissive too – I'd like you to meet her." Adam looked at me, his eyebrows raised in surprise.

"She has a tattoo with the same symbol as my necklace, and I recognized it, so we got chatting. She told me about her relationship with her Dom, and she said I could ask her advice if I ever needed it. I think we could be friends, if that's ok?"

"Of course. It's not a bad idea you having someone else to talk to. I mean you really should be able to ask me anything, but I understand how difficult you find it opening up to me just yet. As long as her Dom is ok with it, then it's fine."

I grinned, hugging him tightly. "Then you'd better make it three hot chocolates, and you can thank her for helping me make your gift at extremely short notice, on Christmas Eve. We'll have whipped cream and marshmallows too please."

I gave Adam a smile and went into Kate's little shop, leaving him to get the drinks. She was working at the desk at the back of the shop, as usual, and after glancing up at the tinkle of the bell over the door, she stood up, and a warm smile spread over her face.

"Zoe! Merry Christmas." She came over and hugged me tightly, and was about to speak when Adam walked in through the door carrying the three insulated cups in a cardboard tray. She must have instantly realized who he was from the way I had described him. I immediately grabbed the hot chocolates, handing one to her. Although still smiling, she dipped her head, her eyes downwards, as a gesture of respect, and spoke softly. "It's a pleasure to meet you, Sir."

"You must be Kate. And please, it's Adam." He held his hand out and she took it, smiling. "I believe I owe you thanks for helping my sub with my Christmas present. It's great." He glanced down to his wrist, indicating the discreet leather band that peeped out from beneath the cuff of his sweater. The tiny beads and bars of silvers spaced along the band spelled out the work MASTER in morse code

"It was a pleasure to help. I enjoyed making something a little different but honestly, it was Zoe that had the idea."

Kate admired my necklace, although she referred to it as my "day collar". I made a mental note to ask Adam what that meant later. He was looking at some of the silver pieces in the cabinets, and Kate went over to him.

"They're all designs of my own, but I'm happy to work with the customer if there is something that they particularly want to incorporate."

"Some of these pieces are really beautiful" Adam replied. "Do you only work in silver?"

"Mainly, yes. It's more forgiving and robust. I do love to work with gold, although that makes a huge difference to the pricing, obviously. I can incorporate gemstones, too, but the customer would have source their own stones. I do have contacts for a couple of reputable lapidaries or gemologists, but any purchase from them would be totally separate. I simply set the stones as part of the design that I work out with the customer."

We all chatted for a while, about Christmas, and her business, and plans after the holidays. Adam asked about her Master – not to pry, but he wanted to make sure that Kate's Dom would be happy about her meeting me for a drink sometime, and agreed he thought it would be useful for me to have someone to talk to – to ask any questions I might have, or get a female perspective. Then dropping his cup into the waste bin in the corner, he slipped his arm around my waist.

"Well, it was good to meet you, Kate. I'm sure I'll see you again. Come on love, let's go and find something to eat. The lunchtime rush should be over by now."

I turned to Kate, who gave me a quick hug. "We should go out for that drink soon. Give me a call anytime. And thanks for the hot chocolate."

"Will do… as soon as things settle down at work in the New Year, I promise. Bye lovely."

We headed to the Italian bistro just a few minutes stroll from Kate's little shop, and the smell of garlic and rosemary suddenly made me feel famished. We shared a selection of olives and chunks of bread, dipped in oil and balsamic vinegar. Adam ordered chargrilled chicken with apricots and mustard in a creamy sauce with penne, while I chose a risotto with chorizo, goats' cheese and roasted cherry tomatoes, finished with pine nuts. We shared a house salad, and a bottle of sparkling water.

"Kate seems really nice." Adam said an hour later, as our coffees arrived, served with amaretti biscuits wrapped in pretty gold paper.

"She is" I agreed, "And I just love some of the stuff she makes. I've told her, I don't know why she isn't selling her designs to high end jewellers in London or somewhere. That reminds me, what did she mean when she referred to my necklace as a day collar? I know that you call it a collar, and I understand what that infers, but why *day* collar specifically?"

"Well, it's because to most people it isn't obviously a collar. I mean it us just a pretty necklace to anyone who doesn't recognize the significance of the symbol. Kate's collar is more like what you once referred to as a dog collar. Have you seen the the locking clasp at the back? I bet she doesn't have the key to that. Then there's the ring at the front. That's another type of symbol. It's taken from an erotic book written in the early 1950's called 'The Story of O'. It was one of the first published to explore the themes of dominance and submission. It was banned for years."

I sipped my coffee, cocking my head to one side in interest, and Adam continued.

"It's set in France. The main character, known only as 'O' is sent by her lover to a chateau in Roissy, where she's trained as a submissive to serve members of a secret society there. She has a metal collar fastened around her neck with a ring at the front, and often there are chains attached to it, and the shackles on her wrists. The style your friend Kate wears is known as a "ring of O". I doubt you'd get away with wearing something like that to work without raising a few eyebrows, so your 'day collar' is something far more discreet. It is more a representation of a collar; you have the ability to take it off, rather than it being something more permanent."

"Okaaay… so I've got to wear it at weekends, and when we're together, but you haven't said whether I am allowed to wear it at other times. I mean, am I allowed to wear it for work? Or is it only when I'm with you? There seem to be so many rules."

"That's up to you sweetheart. I don't want you to feel I have taken away all your freedom. Not yet anyway. You need to be who you are and do what you do at work. I may want to control you at home, but I certainly don't want to stop you having a life outside of us, if that makes sense. This is *my* game, and I don't want to force you to play it seven days a week."

"But what if I want to wear it. Are you saying I can't?" Adam paid the bill, and we headed back outside, making our way back toward the carpark.

"No, of course not. You just need to understand that when you are wearing it, your behaviour should be that of a sub. My sub. Everything you do and say when you are wearing my collar reflects on me, whether you are with me or not. If you're at work your focus is on your job. I get that. You don't want to be worrying about how to behave when I'm not around." He took my hand, raising it kiss my knuckles as we walked.

"I'm still confused. I wouldn't behave any differently when you're not around, than when you are?"

"Well, that's partly because I'm not quite so controlling as some Doms are. I don't make you walk a step behind me, or stay at home to cook and clean for me. You're not my slave. That's a different type of D/s dynamic that I don't particularly hold with."

"Damn right!" I said indignantly. "Do you mean some people do actually treat their subs like slaves?"

"They do. It has to be an arrangement that's agreed by both parties and is mutually advantageous. Some women – and men – want to give everything up; to not have to think for themselves at all. They don't have their own money, or responsibilities. Like I said, I don't want our relationship to be like that."

"That's fucking ridiculous – I mean, why would you?" I shook my head, shocked at the idea.

Adam scowled at my choice of words. "It's whatever floats your boat, I guess. There isn't a 'One-Size-Fits-All' in any relationship. All I ask is that when we are in a public space you speak to me respectfully, *don't* use bad language again please, and allow me to take the lead. I mentioned when we were at the beach, you should not speak first to a stranger, but wait for them to address us, and for me to respond, or I will signal that it's ok to speak. Think of it as if you were at school, and how you'd behave in front of your Headmaster."

"I never had kinky sex with my Headmaster." I smiled.

"Ok, bad example. Maybe like a boss that you get on really with. You might talk honestly in private – swear, share banter, a dirty joke maybe. But if you were meeting with important clients, you'd moderate your language, behave in a more proper manner. Be a little more respectful."

We were back at the car now. Adam opened my door and then gave me a quick kiss. "Stop worrying about everything babe. Or have I got to take you over my knee to stop you over-thinking again?"

8

We drove back to Adam's having first called a supermarket to pick up some milk and other essentials. We were both still full from our lunch, so we lazed on the sofa. We watched a film, then put some music on. Later Adam went to have a shower, and I made a quick salad with some cold chicken, a bag of peppery salad leaves and sliced avocado. I peeled and carefully segmented a couple of oranges, putting the flesh into the salad, and reserving the juice, which I used to make a dressing with olive oil and white wine vinegar and a touch of Dijon mustard, and set one side to drizzle over just before we ate. By the time Adam returned freshly showered and smelling gorgeous, I had laid the table and was frying little cubes of ciabatta in garlic oil for some crunch.

"Hmm, you have been busy" he said, wrapping his arms around me from behind, and kissing the back of my neck. I scooped the now crispy croutons onto paper towel to absorb up any excess oil, leaving them to cool for a moment while I turned back to the jar of dressing and gave it a good shake.

"Well, I'm not especially hungry after such a late lunch, but we still need to eat, so I thought I'd just make something light. I hope it's ok. I still don't know everything you like and don't like to eat."

"You mean apart from you, wench?" he growled and bit the side of my neck.

"I suppose I walked right into that." I laughed, ducking away from him, so I could take the salad over to the table.

"I don't need much encouragement around you." Adam went out into the utility room and came back with a bottle. "The overflow fridge" he explained, before pouring two large glass of honey coloured pinot gris, and then joining me at the table.   The wine was delicious, and beautifully balanced the zesty salad, which was pretty good, if I do say so myself. We took our time, chatting and listening to music while we ate, then together we cleared the table, and I stacked the dishwasher. Adam topped up my wine, and we sat on the sofa.

"Is it ok if I have a bath?" I asked, while Adam flicked through the tv channels to find something worth watching.

"Of course. You don't need to ask permission."

"Ok thanks. Won't be too long" I stood to go upstairs.

"Take your wine and have a soak. Are you coming back down, or shall I come up in a while?" he wiggled his eyebrows and gave me a grin.

"Adam Taylor, you've got a one-track mind" I laughed. "I'll shout you when I'm out.

I ran a bath, tying my hair up into a loose bun so I wouldn't have to wash it, then sank up to my neck in bubbles. Adam didn't use the main bathroom because he preferred to shower, and the en-suite had a double width cubicle, with a rainfall head as well as a smaller adjustable hand-held spray, all with fancy digital controls. This bathroom only had a basic mixer shower over the bath, and you could tell no-one had used it. There wasn't so much as a bottle of shampoo in the cabinet, and I'd even had to put a new toilet roll onto the holder.

I lay back for a while, listing to a playlist on my phone, the hot water making me drowsy.

"Knock, knock" Adam stuck his head around the door. "You still alive babe? You've been in there for ages." I opened my eyes with a start at the realisation I'd fallen asleep.

"Sorry, I must have nodded off." I pushed myself upwards in the bath, suddenly aware that the water was no longer hot, and my fingers were pruney. "I'll be out in a min."

"No rush – just making sure you're ok. I'm going to jump in the shower. I shall await your presence in the boudoir in due course." He bowed in mock reverence, backing out of the door and closing it behind him. I washed quickly, shaved my armpits and did a quick tidy-up of my pubic area, then climbed out. Then I sat on the side of the bath and smoothed my favourite Molton Brown body oil over my damp skin - a Christmas gift from an old school friend and far too pricey to justify buying for myself. She lived in Exeter, and although we didn't see each other very often these days, we were still close and always sent each other gifts.

9

Adam climbed into bed next to me and pulled me against him. He stroked his fingers up my arm, my shoulder, kissing me softly all the while. "Hmmm, soft. I like soft." His hand moved to hold the back of my neck as his kisses grew more urgent. He moved down to kiss the side of my neck, then whispered in my ear, "Good enough to eat."

I moaned in response, feeling a sudden heat between my legs, as he feathered kisses across my collar bone, then moved lower to take one of my nipples into his mouth, while his fingers moved to pinch the other. Me breath hitched as he pulled at the tender skin with his teeth, and I reached down to touch him, to pull him closer.

"I think it's time you learned a lesson in control." He raised so he was sitting up on the bed beside me, then threw the bedclothes on the floor. Then he reached down and picked up a towel from the floor at the side of the bed. "Put your hands up on the pillow, either side of your head – or behind your head if you prefer. That's it. Comfortable?"

I nodded, "Yes, comfortable."

"Good girl. Now, you're going to keep your hands there, no matter what. There may not be any ropes or cuffs, but you are going to stay in that position as if you were physically tied, until I tell you otherwise. It's called honour bondage. Spread your legs for me, nice and wide, now close your eyes. And all you have to remember is that your pleasure depends on your own will-power. Is that understood?"

"Yes but…"

"And just one more thing – you don't get to cum until I say so. Tell me when you're getting close, and right before you're about to cum you tell me to stop. I mean it. If you don't, I'll punish you, and I don't just mean a spanking. You enjoy that too much."

I groaned, not sure it sounded like fun any more, but then his mouth was on mine before I got the chance to object. He kissed down to my breasts, then moved lower across my belly and hips. He moved down, positioning himself between my legs. Then, pushing them farther apart, he began to kiss across my hips, kissing all the way down my inner thigh to my knee and back up again. I was breathing faster now, as he got close to my pussy, but then he moved to the other leg. As he moved back upwards, he sucked at the skin on my inner thigh, hard enough that I knew it would leave a mark. Now his mouth was so close I could feel his breath on my pussy lips and lifted my hips to meet his mouth, but he pulled away, suddenly pinching me hard on the inside of my thigh.

"Ow!" I squealed at the unexpected pain, then tried to compose myself again. He kissed either side of my opening, his tongue flicking over my pussy lips with the lightest touch, just teasing, making me whimper. His hand moved up to pinch my nipple as he continued to kiss and lick all around my pussy, still not touching my clit.

Adam put his hands under my legs and pushed my knees up and outwards, spreading me wide open to him. Then using his flat tongue, he licked painfully slowly, starting from the bottom of my vulva, moving up across my slit and finally passing over my clit, making me jolt. He lifted his head then moved back down to do it again and again, his tongue just wide and flat, with just enough pressure that soon I was climbing towards my first orgasm. The action was so slow and steady, and the pressure just enough. I was breathing hard now, trying hard not to tilt my hips up and take what I so desperately wanted.

"Oh god, yes, I'm gonna cum… No!" He stopped licking, and just pressed his tongue against my clit, holding still for a moment, then kissed gently my lips either side of my vagina, my inner thighs, then back up to my breasts, sucking on each nipple in turn.

"That was too close. Remember, you have to tell me when to stop." He nuzzled into my neck, kissing and nibbling my ears and down to my collar bones. "I can feel your pulse racing" he whispered, pressing his lips against the carotid artery in my neck.

He moved down again, lying between my parted thighs, and I whimpered in anticipation as I felt his breath against my outer lips. His tongue moved over my opening, lapping at my juices, then he closed his lips around my clit and began gently sucking it, drawing it into his mouth. I moaned, my hands gripping the pillows either side of my head, as he relaxed his mouth and released the pressure, then sucked again pulling my clit in and out of his mouth, sucking, releasing, sucking, releasing. Soon I was climbing again, racing towards an orgasm, willing it to happen but at the same time praying I could hold it off and prolong this delicious torture. My head tossed from side to side, desperately trying not to move any other part of my body, until the pressure became so intense...

"Stop!" I was panting hard, and whimpered when his mouth left my clit, suddenly deprived of his touch.

"Good girl" he said, and moved back up the bed, leaning down up to kiss my mouth, the tang of my arousal on his tongue. His hand moved over my breasts, then down over my belly to dip between my folds. I flinched as his fingers touched my clit, which was super-sensitive now, and he chuckled. His mouth sucked again at my nipples, and as he did so, my internal muscles clenched. His hand was flat against my pussy now, just cupping me, as if holding me still to steady me, as I gradually calmed down and relaxed again.

After a few moments his hands ran up and down over my thighs, and he moved lower again and began kissing over my abdomen and hips, his hands gripping my bum and lifting me towards him as he moved down, down to where I desperately wanted to feel his mouth. He started gently again, licking from the bottom of my slit agonizingly slowly up to my clit, this time applying more pressure with his tongue. The bundle of nerves was so sensitive that it made me jump as the tip of his tongue flicked over my clit. Then he was sucking again, pulling my swollen bud between his lips, sucking, releasing, sucking. I moaned, mumbling something incoherent, praying for that sweet release. He sucked me into his mouth again, this time holding my aching clit there while the tip of his tongue massaged it.

"Oh god, Adam, please. I'm so close. Please let me cum this time…please." He carried on sucking, licking, as the muscles in my thighs and buttocks clenched and unclenched, desperately fighting the urge to grab his head and grind my pussy onto his mouth.

"No, stop. STOP!" I cried out, pleading with him.

He stopped and smiled up at me, pausing while my breathing slowed just a fraction, but then suddenly his head was back between my legs, and his tongue moved faster now, a steady rhythm back and forth to one side of my clit, just the right pressure. I'd barely come down, and this time I couldn't stop the powerful orgasm as it ripped through me. It felt like every muscle in my body clenched at the same time, my thighs clamped against his face and I screamed my release through gritted teeth, all the while his tongue continued to move, just gently, gently, the pressure so light now, but the rhythm still constant. My hands went to his head, not sure whether to pull him onto me, or push him off. I wasn't sure whether I was laughing or crying when he eventually lifted his head, then pushed himself up to lie by the side of me. I lay panting, my arms outstretched, and he leaned down to kiss me, his lips and beard sticky with my wetness.

"God you're beautiful when you cum. I could eat you all night."

"No, please, I wouldn't survive." I laughed, still trying to catch my breath.

"Oh, I don't know…" He shifted his weight, leaning up on one elbow "I think you can give me one more."

He sat up, moving to the side of me. "This might get messy" he said, moving down between my legs. "Lift up."

"You've got to be kidding me!" I lifted my hips, and he pushed the edge of the towel underneath my bum. Then laying down again against my side, his fingers slipped down between my folds, and into my opening. I moaned as he slid them in and out, up over my clit, then back inside. I began to move my hips to meet the thrust of his fingers, while his thumb pressed my already hyper-sensitive clit. His mouth was on my nipple, his tongue swirling and then he was sucking it hard, until it was almost painful. My arms moved down to his shoulders, my fingers digging in, as suddenly his fingers began to curl against my G-spot. He moved faster and faster, and my inner walls tightened, trying to pull him inside me and I knew I was going to cum again before too long.

"Don't clench, baby. Bear down, push against it."

His fingers pressed rigid against the upper walls of my vagina, his wrist moving up and down so the heel of his hand moved against my clit. It was all too much, the speed of the movement inside me and the pressure building.

"There we go." he said matter-of-factly, as he felt my release, and I couldn't help but cry out, my head and shoulders lifting off the pillows.

"Jesus, fuuuuuckaaaaaaah!" I screamed as my inner muscles spasmed and suddenly I felt like I couldn't breathe. I felt a gush of wetness with each pulse of my inner muscles, and I could hear the squelching sound of his fingers inside my sopping wet cunt. My pussy clenched hard, gripping him. He slowed, then stilled his hand while my pussy continued to pulse with aftershocks, before he eventually withdrew his fingers.

Adam got off the bed and, picking up the towel, went into the en-suite bathroom. He came back with a warm but damp flannel, which he placed against my throbbing pussy, cleaning and gently soothing the area. I sighed, then yawned, suddenly worn out.

"Tired out?" he asked.

"Mm-hmm" I nodded. "Just give me a minute."

He lay down on his back beside me, and I turned towards him, snuggling under his arm, my mouth against his neck. My hand went to his chest, then I stroked down the trail of hair that ran from his belly button down to meet his pubes. As I moved downwards, reaching for his cock, he lifted my hand, curling his fingers into mine and kissing them softly.

"Time for sleep" he said, placing my hand back on his chest and covering it with his own.

"I want to take care of you now." I tried to move, ready to crawl down the bed and take him in my mouth, but he tightened his grip to hold me still.

"I'm fine baby. My pleasure is seeing your pleasure. The look on your face when you come undone, when you give everything to me. Honestly, it's the sexiest thing I've ever seen." He pulled me tight against him, then relaxed, lowering his face to take my mouth. We kissed slowly, his tongue dancing lightly with mine, as if he was tasting me for the first time.

A few moments later I lay in his arms, drifting off to sleep, while he stroked my hair. He spoke softly. "Maybe now you see how good it can be to give up control."

The next morning was grey and miserable, which matched my mood. It was our last day together before we both had to return to the normality of work, and I didn't want it to end. I cooked scrambled eggs and streaky bacon for breakfast, while Adam spooned coffee into a cafetière and poured on the water, then filled two glasses with orange juice. He was in a playful mood and distracted me with a kiss while reaching around to swipe a piece of crispy bacon. It felt nice to be that close, just pottering around his kitchen, doing the ordinary together. We ate at the breakfast bar, the radio on in the background, then I washed the few dishes, and he dried, putting them away while I wiped the work surfaces.

Adam kissed me, then licked his lips, "Mm mmm … bacon My favourite flavour on a woman. What do you want to do today, hot stuff?"

"I don't know. I don't really feel like going out anywhere in this rain. Can we just stay here? Maybe watch a film?"

"Ok, but I need to check my work emails, and I probably should iron a couple of shirts too. Can you amuse yourself for an hour or so while I get that done? You could pop into town and see what you can find in the Sales. I'll drop you off if you like, so you don't have to park, and can pick you up later."

"Nah – I hate shopping." Adam raised an eyebrow. "What? Don't look at me like that. Not all women think of shopping as a leisure pursuit you know. I only go into town if I have to, if I need something I can't get online. I get frustrated in shops which cater to girls in sizes 4-12 and hate the look of horror you get if you ask for something in a size 16. And don't even get me started on shoe shopping when you're a size 9, which even if it is available, no-one ever carries in stock."

"Ok, it was just a suggestion. I tell you what, why don't you use my ipad and see if you can find some places you'd like to go for a break when the weather gets better. I mean, I know I said maybe the lakes, but I'm open to suggestions. That should keep you busy for a while."

"Really? What sort of thing did you have in mind?"

"Honestly sweetheart, it's your choice. I don't really do holidays – never have – so just find a few places you fancy, and you can show me later. We'll book a week, but I don't mind whether it's staying in one place or travelling round a bit. And I'm not bothered whether it's hotels or something else, but just one thing - we are NOT going camping. OK?"

"No problem. Leave it to me." I was suddenly excited to start planning a break together. We would both need to sort out what time we could book when we got back to work, but it was nice to start thinking about where we could go.

Adam went and put the ironing board up in the kitchen-diner and chose an 80's rock mix from his phone, which played from the Bluetooth speakers throughout the ground floor. Before long we were both wailing along to the likes of Gary Moore, ZZ Top, Rainbow and Bon Jovi. I lounged on the sofa, searching holiday accommodation in Devon, and bookmarking a couple of places I liked the look of. I'd spent a couple of years at boarding school in Devon during my teens while my dad worked in Dubai, and also had fond memories of caravan holidays in Swanage and Weymouth. Before long I'd saved the details of a beautiful looking stable conversion on a 100 acre estate near Lyme Regis, and a luxury lakeside lodge set in woodland just outside Exeter which looked equally stunning.

"I'm done" Adam closed his laptop. "The rest can wait until I get to work tomorrow. Stick the kettle on, and I'll just go and hang these up." He stood and gathered the newly ironed shirts which he'd put on hangers on the back of the door and took them up to the bedroom while I made a pot of tea.

"So, where are we going?" He re-appeared in the kitchen, and after grabbing a packet of biscuits from the cupboard, joined me on the sofa. We drank our tea while I showed him the accommodation that I'd saved, and some of the places nearby that I thought we might visit.

"Of the two, I prefer the lodge in the forest," he said, between bites of a digestive, "but I'm really not bothered about a hot tub. I know they're supposed to be romantic and all that, but I've never been able to get enthusiastic about sitting in a vat of human soup. I mean, we'll book one if you want, I know you like to soak, but you won't get me in it."

"Really? I'm sure they clean it all out between guests – they must do. And you have a shower before you get in."

"Nah, I just don't see the point of sitting there in hot water. It just makes me feel hot and bothered, and saps all my energy. I'll just sit beside it and keep your glass topped up. How about June or early July? I'd rather avoid school holidays, but at least the weather will be a bit better by then, fingers crossed."

"Sounds good." I agreed. "I'll have a look at the calendar when I get chance next week, and make a note of some possible dates, then we can get it booked. Hopefully I can get a couple of new staff before then, but I really could to with someone at a level I can train to cover my job while I'm away."

"I thought that fella Chris was going to do a bit more? Or is that not working out?"

Chris was one of the Call Centre staff, but he'd spent the last six months reminding everyone that he had a business degree, and so was wasted on the phones. I'd finally agreed to give him some training on the data reporting parts of my job, and he was now producing some of the weekly management figures to free up a bit of my time.

"It's helped a bit, but it's not great. He thinks he's some sort of supervisor, and it's causing friction with others in the team. If only he'd spend as much time working as he does bigging himself up to everyone who'd listen. Honestly, he's just cherry-picking the bits he wants to do, that make him look good, so he can talk the talk with the management. His people skills are shit, and the rest of the guys are just getting pissed off with his attitude."

"You'll figure it out. You need to get a Supervisor or Team Leader. Someone that has a dedicated role, instead of being neither one thing nor another. He probably struggles with knowing what's expected of him."

"Hmmm, maybe. Anyway, forget work. And put those bloody biscuits away! If you're hungry I'll make some proper food. What do you want for lunch?"

Having decided it was a soup kind of day, Adam nipped out to the bakery just around the corner to get some fresh crusty bread. I put a tub of fresh tomato and basil into a saucepan to heat up, then peeled and chopped some fruit salad for afterwards, mixing a bit of honey with Greek yoghurt to dollop on top.   He was back within a few minutes with a granary cob which was still warm inside and smelled delicious when I cut it into thick chunks for with the soup.

After lunch, we settled on the sofa and watched the 1951 classic "Scrooge". The black and white version with Alistair Sim in the lead role was, to my mind, the best version ever made. Adam tried his best to convince me that it wasn't as good as the Muppet Christmas Carol, but by the end he did agree that the haunting chill of the wind and the fear in the eyes of the quaking Scrooge brought far more drama and darkness to Dickens' original story than Gonzo and Kermit ever could - even with help from Michael Caine.

Later that afternoon, I went and packed may bag. We were both back at work the next morning, and I wanted to have everything sorted so we could enjoy our last evening then have an early night. I was only going to be in for three days before we closed again for the New Years weekend, so I'd told the staff that they could dress down. I was glad I'd be able to just put my jeans, sweater and boots on in the morning, rather than my usual dress or trouser suit with heels.

"Why don't you leave some stuff here?" Adam had asked. "You are coming back at the weekend, aren't you?"

"Well yes, but I need to do some washing. Besides, you said you're going to be late on Friday night, so I thought if you're tired, you'd rather I came over on Saturday."

"I'd hoped you'd be here waiting for me when I get in on Friday night. That's why I gave you the key. And when I said late, I should be back in time for dinner – probably around eight-ish, or not long after. I'll pick up a takeaway on the way home." He pulled me in for a kiss, then nuzzled against my neck, a smile in his voice as he growled "I like the idea of coming home to a cold beer and a hot woman."

"In that order? Thanks. It's good to know what your priorities are."

11

That evening we went out, walking along the canal into the heart of town. It was fairly quiet, with most people still at celebrating Christmas at home, or visiting family. There was always a bit of a lull between the building up to the festivities and the Christmas Eve party atmosphere, and the madness of New Years Eve a week later. We both fancied a steak, and decided to try our luck at one of the better restaurants, who said they could seat us in about half an hour, if we wanted to go for a drink somewhere and come back.   Having agreed that we were happy with that, we went and had a glass of wine at the pub a few doors down.

The meal was well worth the wait. Adam had the goats cheese ciabatta with Cumberland sauce, and I had a stilton, pear and walnut salad to start. We both then had a fillet steak, Adam choosing to top his with streaky bacon and melting stilton with a port jus, while I opted for a creamy sauce of garlic, mushrooms and Marsala. The hand cut beef dripping chips were fantastic. We shared a bottle of Shiraz, and talked about the holiday, then conversation turned to work. I loved my job, but this was our busiest time of the year, and we really needed some more staff.

We decided to skip the coffee, as it was already getting late, so walked home, both feeling full and sleepy.

"Straight to bed, wench. And none of your naughtiness tonight, either!" he smiled, swatting me on the backside. "We've both got to be up early."

"Hah! *My* naughtiness? How very dare you!" I laughed as we climbed the stairs.

"Hey listen, I know I'm irresistible, and as soon as I get my clothes off, you turn into a sex crazed animal, but you'll just have to control yourself."

"Hmmm – you mean you wish!"

We were soon in bed, and he wrapped me up for a cuddle before we both set the alarms on our respective phones, and I turned onto my side. Within a few minutes, I could hear the change in Adam's breathing, and I knew he was asleep.

12

The next morning, I had been concerned about oversleeping and being late for work, but I was awake just before the alarm went off at 6:45. I needn't have worried. Just a few minutes later, Adam appeared in the bedroom doorway with a cup of coffee.

"Hey, beautiful." He sat on the edge of the bed and gave me a quick peck. His hair was freshly washed, and he was wearing smart blue shirt and grey trousers.

"Thanks. I didn't hear you get up?"

"I didn't want to wake you. I thought I'd check my emails before I leave, but I'm heading off in a min. Help yourself to breakfast, and I'll talk to you later. Listen, I'm gonna be really busy today, so if you text me, don't worry if I don't answer straight away." He stood up to leave. "I'll give you a ring tonight when I'm home. Have a good day."

"You too, sweetheart" I replied, and with that he headed off downstairs.

A few minutes later I heard him close the front door and start his car. I showered quickly, then finished my coffee while I got dressed. I quickly rinsed my cup, grabbed my bags, and pulled the front door closed behind me. I wasn't looking forward to getting to work, because it was always so very busy after the Christmas period, with delivery problems, and returns, and of course the post Christmas sale, all of which meant a leap in call volumes. I might have to ask people to work through their breaks, but I had recently implemented flexible hours, so people could "bank" up to an hour a day to use at another time.

When I pulled into the carpark, Chris Collins was waiting by the front door. He stood aside while I unlocked the door, then followed me as I moved through the building turning lights on.

"Did you have a nice Christmas?" he asked, hovering in front of my desk.

"Yes thanks" I replied, "Quiet." I smiled to myself, thinking of the last few days of kinky-fuckery which had been anything *but* quiet. I turned on my PC and the two screens that enabled me to monitor the number of calls coming in, and then clicked on my emails, but he was still loitering, looking decidedly uncomfortable. "Was there something you wanted?"

"Er, yes, I was hoping we could have a chat. Talk about my progression. I was hoping I could use my skills and experience to take on more of a supervisory role – I mean I know you've been talking about hiring a Team Leader for a while now, and…"

"Chris, I'm really sorry, but now isn't the time. We're in the middle of the busiest time of the year, the calls are going to be queueing all day, and I just need you on the phone at the moment. I can do the figures for a couple of weeks, then we'll review things. I appreciate your help with some of the admin, but I thought you were just enjoying having a break from the phone for a while each day. I hope you didn't read too much into it." He looked crestfallen, and a little angry, so I did my best to smooth his feathers. "I'm certainly looking to recruit very soon, and whether it is a supervisor, or someone to take on some training on the admin, I'm not sure yet. As soon as I figure it out, I'll let you know so you can let me have a CV."

I got up and walked away before he had the chance to respond, and headed over to the coffee machine, where a few of the staff had gathered. The room was filling up and there was a hum of lively conversation, while people compared stories about Christmas presents, family dramas, and who had got the most drunk. By the time I'd got my double espresso from the machine, Chris was at his desk, headset on, and scowling at the screen waiting for the phones to be turned on and the calls to start.

13

The next couple of days were a blur. We were so busy, I ate lunch at my desk, trying to answer emails and deal with Customer Service queries, while constantly shouting "Calls waiting!" and "Get off wrap up" until I was sick of the sound of my own voice. As each called ended, the system built in an automatic wrap up time of 20 seconds to put any notes on the customer account, before feeding the next waiting call through. I'd cut the wrap-up time to 15 seconds, then 12, but still calls were stacking up. The guys on the phone also had an option to take their own line out of the queue, by clicking a button which gave them a bit more time to sort out a more difficult query, or ask some advice, or even just to nip to the loo. They then had to click the same button to be available again, which sometimes they took advantage of, or just accidentally-on-purpose forgot to make themselves available again.

"Come on guys, 12 waiting, and we're getting calls dropping out!" I shouted across the room. "There's a bottle of prosecco or a six-pack of beer the highest call taker between now and Friday." A bit of bribery never hurt, and sure enough, wrap ups became shorter, as did the call queues.

The call centre was only open 8:30 to 5:00 each day, Monday to Friday, but I was there just before 8am to open the building and was usually the last to leave. I tried not to work too late, but often carried on answering emails until around 6:00pm, just because I could get so much more done when the phones were off. The problem was, while I kept doing extra hours just to get my job done, it had been difficult to persuade the MD that I needed to recruit some help. Doing unpaid overtime wasn't helping the situation, but it was hard for me not to give my all to something, or to admit I wasn't managing.

The business was doing well, and I had the go-ahead for 5 more call takers, and one at a slightly higher lever, be it Call Centre Team Leader, or something similar. I was already thinking that a couple of the older more experienced staff would be better suited to a Customer Service role, and could deal with the letters and email queries, or take calls that warranted escalation. I could then recruit inexperienced staff to train as call handlers, just taking orders and payments, and maybe have a dedicated payments line. Obviously, Chris had presumed he would step up, but to be honest, he was just not the right fit. He always had such a high opinion of himself, and was constantly bragging about his business degree meaning he had letters after his name. The rest of the staff already thought he was up Managements' arse, his people skills were non-existent, and basically no-one liked him. Not that making friends should be important to a team leader or supervisor, but if he were to be promoted, they would have absolutely no respect for him, and it would surely lead to bad feeling within the team. Still, I wouldn't have the time to sort out advertising the vacancies, let alone deal with interviews, for at least a week or so after the New Year.

I was too busy to text or call Adam in the day, but we spoke most evenings. He was stuck at work quite late too, so on Thursday he didn't call me until 9:30, just as I was about to have before an early night.

"Hey sexy, sorry its late. What are you up to?" I could tell from his voice that he was tired.

"Well, I'm naked, and up to my neck in bubbles if you really want to know" I replied. "Are you ok? You sound tired. Had a tough day?"

"You could say that." he yawned. "One of my drivers was in an accident on the M5. There was another vehicle involved and the car driver is badly hurt, so I've been dealing with the police all day, after having to get another driver and tractor unit down to pick up the trailer and make the delivery, then sorting out disgruntled customer, and of course getting the driver back home after he was interviewed and the police released him."

"Oh god, that sounds awful. Was the car driver seriously injured? Do you know whose fault it was?"

"He's in hospital, and suffered injuries to his legs from what I can tell, but nothing life changing. The vehicles all have telematics now, so the police have all the information they need to help with investigating the cause. The truck driver claims the car was in the middle lane, and cut across in front of him, because he'd almost missed the junction, but the tail clipped the front of the truck, and he spun off, ending up down the embankment. Our driver was a little shaken. The drink and drugs screens came up negative, thankfully, but we'll have to do our own internal investigation. It's such a ball-ache. You wouldn't believe the amount of paperwork I've got to get through. I'm going to be here until bloody midnight."

"Don't stay too late, you're not going to be productive if you're that knackered. Go home, get some sleep, and crack on with it when you're rested. You'll be thinking more clearly in the morning."

"You're probably right, but I need to get the initial accident report logged before I finish tonight. How was your day – still busy?

"Yeah, I had to resort to bribery and corruption to get the call speeds up, but it seems to have worked today. Chris and Megan were neck and neck on total calls answered at the end of today, so it's all to play for tomorrow. There's nothing like a bit of healthy competition to focus people, and if all it costs me is a bottle of cheap fizz or a couple of beers, it's all good."

"Ok, well I need to get this paperwork sorted. Enjoy your bath and get an early night. I'm still hoping to get away by 7:30 or thereabouts tomorrow, but if it's going to be any different, I'll let you know. If you don't hear otherwise, I'll grab a takeaway, and see you just about 8."

"Ok, sounds good. I'll be waiting with the cold beer."

"You'd better be, wench. And be warned, after the few days I've had, I may have some tension to work out on you. Night sexy." He chuckled as he hung up the phone, but I wasn't sure how serious he was, and that made me nervous. I was still getting used to my new role as Adam's Sub.

14

On Friday evening, I left work on time, so that I could go home and get a few things together before heading over to Adam's house. I'd just walked in, when my mobile started ringing, and the caller ID showed it was Angela, my old school friend.

"Ange, how are you? Long time no speak." We had shared a room at boarding school when we were in the sixth form, and we had been good friends ever since.

"Not great" she sighed. "Have you got time to talk? I'm not interrupting anything am I?"

"No of course not. I'm going out later, but I've got plenty of time. What's up?" There was a pause before she sighed, then answered.

"Me and Mark are splitting up. It's not been right for a while, but things came to a head of Christmas, and we've decided to call it a day."

"Oh babe, I'm so sorry. Are you sure you can't fix things? I mean Christmas is always stressful, with families, and stuff to deal with. What's happened? Has he been cheating?"

"No nothing like that. I think we just want different things. He keeps banging on about wanting to start a family, and I'm not ready. I don't know whether I ever want kids, and he thinks I'm being selfish, because his mum isn't going to get any grandkids if we don't, what with his sister being gay, and in her 50s now. He seems to think it's our duty or something." She paused, and I heard her take a swig from her drink. "It's been coming for a while now, but I suppose we both had too much too drink and a few home truths came out. We've been together since Uni, and we just aren't the same people anymore. Neither of us is really happy, so we've agreed to call it a day."

"That's such a shame. I thought you guys would be together forever. What are you going to do, I mean about the house and stuff? Is he moving out?"

"No. He put a big deposit down with some money his gran left him, but the mortgage has always been in joint names. He says he doesn't want to sell, because it's so handy for work, but we haven't really worked out the details yet. We'll have to get it valued and see if he can afford to buy me out."

"It's really sad, but if it's what you both want, then of course you need to do what makes you happy babe. Is there anything I can do?" Ange had been amazing when I divorced almost four years earlier. She had been on the end of the phone when I was crying and drunk in the middle of the night, or had calmed me down when I was calling me ex all he names under the sun and smashing all the crockery and glasses that we had bought together from Ikea. We didn't see each other very often these days, but she had always been the person that I had relied on when I needed anything, whether it was advice, or just someone to listen.

"Well, actually I'd booked a weekend in Bath for Mark's birthday next week, and I can't get a refund, so I was wondering if you were up for a girly weekend? The room is paid for, but it's a spa hotel so we could have a couple of treatments, before hitting the town for some cocktails? Or we could just re-live our youth - get shitfaced on cider and black, cry about boys, throw up in the gutter, then end up in bed together, like we used to."

Soon we were both laughing and reminiscing about sneaking out of our boarding house at weekends to buy cider, and about losing our virginity; her in a classroom after a sixth form ball, me in a cornfield on the edge of the school estate, after climbing out of the study room window late one night to meet a boy.

"I'll have to check with Adam. I just want to make sure he hasn't made any plans for us, but I'm sure it will be fine. Email me the details of the hotel and I'll look at whether it's as easy to get the train down. At least then I won't be worried about how much I drink on the Saturday night, if I'm not driving home on Sunday. And in the meantime, call me if you need anything, or just someone to talk to. I know it's going to be hard, even if it is mutual. You've got a lot to sort out and there are bound to be some tears and tantrums along the way."

"Thanks Zoe – I don't know what I'd do without you to talk to sometimes. Speak soon babe. Love you."

"Love you too. Take care of yourself."

I sat for a few moments after we ended the call, just thinking about Ange and Mark, and what had always seemed from the outside to be the perfect relationship. They had met at University in Warwick, when Ange was studying English Literature, and he was in his final year of Law. He had ended up working on the legal team for a large insurance firm in Exeter, and when Ange had finished uni, and found that there was no dream job waiting for her, she moved in with Mark, and took a job in the same law firm, as a claims handler – "just until something better comes along". She had moved around various departments, including a stint doing admin for the HR department, and was now a Manager and Trainer in the insurance call centre. I wondered if it was going to be practical to still both work for the same company, although I was fairly sure they didn't even work in the same building, so would be unlikely to run in to each other very often.

I dived into a quick shower to wash off the day, shoved a few things into my overnight bag, put some laundry into the washing machine and turned that on, then left for Adam's place.

15

"Of course you should go." Adam drained the last mouthful of his bottle of beer, then got up to fetch another from the fridge. "It sounds like she needs friend right now. Why would you think I'd mind?"

"I don't know, I just wanted to check. I didn't know if I needed permission I suppose. As your sub, I mean. I don't know how these things work." I looked down at my hands, suddenly embarrassed.

"Hey," he said, tilting my chin up "It's good that you asked, but I don't own you. And I don't want to rule your life. Angela was in it long before I was, so of course your loyalty is to her right now. When are you going?"

"Next weekend. I think she said the booking is for Friday and Saturday night, but I don't know if I could get the Friday off. I may have to go down on Saturday morning."

"Rubbish. You're entitled to use your leave, just like everyone else. You've got to stop putting the Company first, and imagining you owe them anything. Let's face it, if you dropped dead tomorrow, they'd soon have someone else in your seat."

"Wow, how to make a person feel good." I frowned. "I know you're right, but if I leave Chris to cover for me, he'll be swinging his bollocks around and pissing people off. Megan covered for me last time I was off, but if I ask her, Chris will just spit his dummy out and disrespect her, and she'll have a really hard time."

"So put them both - or neither of them - in charge. Surely you can ask them both to do different tasks, just for the sake of one day, but make it clear they've got to work together. Just book the bloody day off and stop worrying that the place will fall apart without you. And in the meantime, you'd better hurry up and decide what sort of person you want to recruit, and get advertising."

He was right of course, and I gave him a kiss, as I stood to clear away the takeaway cartons. I put the plates in the dishwasher, and turned it on to rinse, then gathered up the cartons and put them into the carrier bag and tied the top.

"Here, I'll put that straight into the dustbin, so it doesn't smell." Adam took the bag from me and dropped it in the bin just outside the back door, before locking it again, while I rinsed the plates.

"You know, you could do something out there – make it a bit prettier? Maybe just a couple of pots or raised planters, and something to climb up the fence.

Then you could get a little table and a couple of chairs, maybe grow some herbs for cooking. Just a thought."

"I've never had a garden; I wouldn't know what to do with one. That's one of the reasons why I bought this place. It isn't big enough to worry about, so I just got the builder to put the slabs down. I don't have the time for looking after plants, and I'd probably kill everything."

"That's a shame, it would be nice to have somewhere to sit and have a beer on a summers evening. And maybe you could even open this blind, let some light into the kitchen, and have something to look at while you're doing the dishes."

"I suppose so – I never had anyone to sit out there with. Besides, I like the dark, and I don't want people looking in. But if you want to take it on, go for it. Either tell me what you need me to buy, or if you want to plant up some pots, just keep a track of what I owe you." He moved towards me, wrapped his arms around me, and gave me that hungry look that made me go weak at the knees. "But right now, the last thing on my mind is gardening."

"Well then Sir, just what *do* you have on your mind?"

His mouth was on mine, one hand went to the back of my head, holding me to him, while the other was around my waist, pulling my hips against his. He kissed me hard, his teeth rough against my lips, and when I eventually pulled away, I was gasping for breath, my heart racing.

"I was just thinking I need to be balls deep inside you. Now."

Adam took my hand and led me back through the open plan lounge area, and I presumed, towards the stairs that led to his bedroom. But instead, he stopped and began kissing me again, his hands moving over my clothes, pulling the hem of my shirt from the waistband of my jeans, before hurriedly unfastening the buttons. My hands were on the back of the sofa to steady myself, then he undid my jeans and yanked them down over my hips before I'd even registered what he was doing.

"Oh!" was all I had time to say, before he spun me around and pushed me so that I fell forward over the back of the sofa, with my hands on the seat to stop myself falling. He pulled at the lace shorts, dragging them down to join my jeans, which were bunched around my knees, and slid his hand between my legs, pushing his fingers inside me. "Ow! Adam, please!"

"Please what?" he was kneading my backside, then he brought his hand down with a hard slap against my right bum cheek. I gasped, then bit my lip, trying not to cry out. The sharp sting faded and was quicky replaced with a warm glow, then he was grinding his pelvis against me, and I could feel the bulge in his trousers nestling against the crack of my arse. He reached down to grab my breasts, pulling me up to standing again, then began kissing and sucking at my neck, while his hands pulled at my nipples. I gasped at the sharp pain as he plucked and pinched them, then cried out loud as he sank his teeth into the muscle at the base of my neck. His hand moved between my legs again, but this time I was soaking wet, and he slid his fingers easily inside me.

"You really are a dirty girl, aren't you?" he said, as he unfastened is trousers, and positioned his cock against my opening. "Well, are you?"

"Yes" I panted, suddenly as desperate as he was.

"Yes what?" he spanked me again, across the other cheek this time.

"Ow. Yes Sir," I moaned. "I'm a dirty girl." He thrust upwards, burying himself inside me in one hard stroke. I cried out, feeling my pussy stretch around his hardness. The position with my jeans around me knees meant I couldn't open my legs very wide, and he felt like a really tight fit inside me. Adam pressed his hand on my back, pushing me down again, so to weight on my arms again, although it meant I was raised up on my tip toes. He began to move inside me, each thrust hard and deliberate, and he let out a grunt every time he slammed into me. The angle meant he was hitting my g-spot with every stroke. His fingers were digging into my hips, pulling me on to his cock, and I knew I would have the bruises to show for it tomorrow.

"Fuck, that's good!" he said, as he began to speed up. "I love the view when I'm fucking you like this." His hands gripped my arse cheeks, spreading them wide open. Then he spat, dripping saliva onto me, and stroked a wetted finger down my cleft, before pushing it inside my sphincter. I gasped at the intrusion. He had taken me with a butt plug inside me before, but somehow this felt more intimate.

"You know I want to take you here" he said, a second finger pushing inside me now. "Not yet, but soon. And you'll beg me for it."

I was shaking my head, my brain telling me I didn't want this, that it was wrong. And yet I could feel myself climbing towards an orgasm, unable to control what was happening to my body. Adam's cock was thrusting hard and fast, and he was panting with the effort, while his finger moved in and out of my asshole. Then he added a second finger and I moaned, not sure whether it was in pain or pleasure.

"Cum with me" he gasped, and as if I'd waited for the command, I did just that. I cried out as my inner muscles gripped around both his cock and his fingers, while my thighs and shoulders burned with the effort of holding me up. Adam let out a loud grunt, as he buried himself again as deep as he could and emptied his balls inside me. My walls pulsed around him, and he twitched, with a sharp intake of breath, then froze again, locked inside me.

We stayed still for a few moments, but then he slipped from me, and I felt our combined fluids running down my thighs. He pulled me up to standing once more, wrapping his arms around me and kissing my shoulders and neck, tenderly this time. We were both drenched with sweat, and I shivered as I cooled down.

"Come on" he said, turning me around, and tucking a lock of damp hair behind my ear. "Let's get you showered and into bed."

I stepped out of my jeans and knickers, before using the underwear to wipe some of the sticky mess from my thighs, while Adam tucked himself back into his boxers, and went to the kitchen for a glass of cold water. He downed it in one, before re-filling the glass, then turning out the lights.

16

We showered together, the water easing away the ache in my shoulders and legs, while Adam's hands covered my skin with scented shower oil. I'd had always enjoyed sex, but this was something I'd never experienced before. I had no idea it could be so all-encompassing.

"You ok?" Adam kissed me on the forehead. "Was I a bit rough?"

"Um, I think so … ok I mean." I felt the blush rising from my chest to my face. "It was just so… intense. I thought I was going to pass out! What's so funny?" Adam was grinning at me.

"Nothing, honest" he smiled. "You're just so amazing. I just struggle to keep my composure and be the bad-ass Dom around you sometimes."

"Don't worry, I won't tell anyone. And yes, it was … something."

"Something, eh? As in something you enjoyed, or something that freaked you out?"

I shrugged, still trying to decide myself. "I was a bit freaked out, I suppose, but it's the idea of it being dirty, you know … there. When I stopped thinking about it, it was good." I was blushing again. "Really good."

Adam turned off the shower and reached out to grab two towels from the heated rail. He tied one around his waist, then draped the other around my shoulders, pulling me into his arms to wrap me in a bear hug.

"God, I fucking love you wench!" We stood in the bathroom, me in his arms, while he swayed as if rocking a child. I felt warm, and safe, and more loved than I ever had. I lay my head against his damp chest and enjoyed the feeling. I was suddenly exhausted and tried unsuccessfully to stifle a yawn. I dried myself off, cleaned my teeth, and stumbled towards the bed. I lay on my side, while Adam snuggled against me, and smiled to myself as I closed my eyes.

17

"You know you could talk to Kate" Adam said, as he poured the coffee the next morning.

"What was that?" I replied absently, while buttering my toast.

"You should talk to Kate. About anal." Now he'd got my attention.

"You're joking, why would I do that? She'd think I was a weirdo, and never want to speak to me again! I'm not telling Kate you want to do that sort of stuff."

"Sweetheart, it may surprise you to know, but 'that sort of stuff' is perfectly normal, and a lot of couples really enjoy it. I'm just saying if you find it difficult talking to me about it, maybe another woman's perspective might help. She's a sub too, and I'll bet you a pound to a penny she either does, or has done, anal. It was just a suggestion. And stop frowning – you'll get wrinkles."

"I'm not sure. I mean how do you even start a conversation like that? *'Hey, do you want a coffee? And by the way, how do you feel about bum sex?'* Right, that'd work."

Adam laughed. "Why don't you text her and ask if you can drop in at the shop today, and if she's got a few minutes to chat? I can drop you off, go and get some grocery shopping, then pick you up later. She did say just ask if you needed any advice, didn't she?"

I thought about it for a few minutes. "Well, she did text me this week, to say she'd done some new stuff with seashell designs. I could drop in and just see how busy she is, or maybe arrange to meet up in the week.

An hour later, Adam dropped me at the entrance to the garden centre and retail village, and said he'd text me when he was on his way back. It had started to rain, so I half ran to her little shop, trying to keep under the cover of the trees and shop awnings as much as possible. It didn't really work, and my wet hair was plastered to my head when I burst in through her door.

"Oh god, Zoe you're soaked. Here!" she grabbed a tea-towel from the little kitchenette at the back of the shop and threw it to me. "Sit here, by the heater, I'll be back in a sec." She motioned for me to sit behind her desk, where there was a warm air heater, then dashed out of the shop door. Two minutes later she re-appeared with what had become our customary hot chocolate, from the kiosk a few doors away. "That'll warm you up!" she grinned.

I thanked her and we both sat and drank, while she showed me the sketches of the new jewellery, and some samples of things she had been working on. There were spirals like snail shells, and some more the shape of ammonites, as well as tiny delicate silver starfish, and seahorses.

"Oh wow, they're gorgeous!" I exclaimed. "I love anything to do with the sea, but these are beautiful and so realistic – not like some of the tacky stuff you get in seaside souvenir shops." My favourite was a silver chain with what looked like a miniature oyster shell, but it was hinged and inside was a tiny seed pearl.

"Choose one – anything. A gift from me."

"Oh no, I couldn't. This is your living, after all. You can't go giving stuff away! Besides, as much as I love the little oyster, I suppose I should stick with earrings really – I don't want to wear anything else when I have this on." I touched the necklace, or day collar, that Adam had given me.

"Of course. How about these then?" She went over to the cabinet and took out a pair of silver drop earrings that had the same intricate triskelion design as the necklace I was wearing. "I tried to remember the proportions of the design on your collar. Yep, they look like a good match." She held them up beside the pendant, before wrapping them in pink tissue and dropping them into a gift bag.

"They're perfect. Thank you so much!" I gave her a tight hug.

"You're welcome, lovely. It's nice to have a friend who gets the relationship I'm in, without judging. I've had to be a bit careful of what I've said in front of girlfriends in the past. How's it going with Adam, by the way?"

"It's great – amazing. He's so different to anyone I've been with before. And don't just mean the kinky stuff. He's kind, and loving, and he makes me feel like a princess, but without stifling me. I just love spending time with him, but love that we still have our own space too. And he's the most generous lover I've ever had. I mean he's not like the guys that just want to shoot their load, and either don't know how to get you off, or worse, don't actually care. He likes it a bit rough, but then still wants to spend so much more time on *my* pleasure."

"And so he should do." she replied. "My Master, Lee, may like to control me physically, but he reminds me that I hold the power at the end of the day. I chose to submit to him and give up my control. I trust him with my life, and I can't give any more than that." I must have looked puzzled, and she went on. "Not every woman is strong enough to be the submissive one in a relationship. And not every man is strong enough to balance the power dynamic. He'll love the thrill of you giving up control, of the basic human impulse to avoid pain and danger. He'll love the strength it takes to bare yourself to him, body, mind and soul. You hold all the cards, babe, but if he's a good Dom, he'll want you to fly." She squeezed my hand.

"Can I ask you something? I mean I don't want to take up too much of your time or anything."

"Babe, there's not been a soul in here all morning. No-one's got any money after Christmas, and the rain is keeping people away. What's up?"

"It's a bit personal … about the physical stuff." I paused, not sure what to say next.

"Honestly, just spit it out babe, you won't shock me." She looked at me expectantly. "Whatever it is, I've probably seen it or done it at least once."

"Well... I wanted to ask you how you feel about anal." There, I'd said it. "Adam wants me to do it, and I don't think I can. It takes me all my time to even say the word!" I was probably bright red in the face, but she just smiled.

"Soooo, when you say anal, he wants to do you? Or wants you to do him?"

"Oh Christ, no! At least I don't think so – he's not mentioned me doing it to him. He wants to do it to me. I just can't understand why he'd want to put his dick in my bum-hole, or why he'd imagine I'd enjoy it. It's just so gross!"

"Is it? I mean you swap saliva, and all your other bodily fluids. You suck his dick I presume; take his cum in your mouth maybe? Isn't that gross? It's a hole at the end of the day, and believe me, it can be really pleasurable too. As long as you build up to it slowly, and are really relaxed, it shouldn't be painful. Maybe just a bit the first time - like losing your virginity."

I shook my head. "Someone did it to me a long time ago, and I couldn't sit down for days. It felt like he'd torn my insides out with a crochet hook – I bled afterwards, and it was excruciating the first time I had to go to the loo – you know, for a poo."

"When you say 'did it to you', I take it your boyfriend was more keen on the idea than you were?"

"He wasn't a boyfriend. Just someone I'd met at a party. I'd had far too much to drink, and he took advantage." I paused, swallowing hard. "I felt ill, and just wanted to lie down, so I told him I was on my period, to put him off, but he decided he'd 'go in the back door' as he put it."

"Oh hun, no wonder you aren't keen. Did you report him? He should have been locked up for rape!"

Of course I hadn't done. I was ashamed, and hurt, and I just wanted to go home and lie in a bath to ease the pain. And I didn't even know his name, or where he had come from, and I felt it was somehow my fault for flirting with him earlier in the evening – like I'd somehow encouraged him.

"Does Adam make you feel like that?"

"No, of course not. He's gentle and kind, and he promises he'll go slowly. He gave me a butt plug a while ago, and after I'd tried it on my own and got a bit used to it, he did put it in me when we had sex once. That was ok."

I was blushing again, and fiddling with the zip on my coat, but Kate encouraged me to go on. "Last night he bent me over the sofa and was fucking me from behind. He got a bit carried away, and he put his fingers in me. He said he wanted to take me there."

"And how did it feel? Did it hurt? I take it he used plenty of lube?" she asked.

"No, actually - just spit. It was kind of gross really, but I didn't get chance to say anything. We were both caught up in the moment, and when I came, he was fucking my pussy, with two fingers in my bum at the same time."

"Okay, so you did orgasm then? I mean something must have felt good, or that wouldn't have happened, right?"

"It wasn't painful or anything. It made me feel really… full? Like well and truly stuffed in fact. He isn't massive, but it felt like he was at that moment. I did enjoy that part I suppose."

"But…?"

"I don't know. It still felt kind of wrong. You know, dirty. Especially the spit thing. And having his cock up there is bound to feel way more painful than a little butt plug, or even two fingers. I don't think he put them in very far – I'm not sure."

"You know he loves you, and the last thing he'd ever want to do is cause you real pain. Why don't you talk to him about how you feel, and maybe try a slightly bigger butt plug? It's perfectly normal to feel anxious about trying something which feels so alien, but honestly babe, all you've got to remember is to relax, be absolutely ready for it, not feel pressured, and use loads of lube. Go slowly, and just try it. If it's painful, or you don't like it you say stop. I presume you have safe words?" I nodded. "Adam isn't the type of guy that's going to tie you up and up and fuck you in the arse without consent. Unless you find that you really love it, of course. Some of us do."

"Really?" I was more than a little surprised, but Kate told me she actually loved anal, whether it was Lee's cock inside her ass, or a dildo in there while he fucked her pussy or used something else to make her cum.

My phone chirped just then, with a message from Adam to say he'd be on the car park in five minutes. I gave Kate a tight squeeze and thanked her for her advice.

"Don't be daft. What are friends for?" she replied. "And don't forget these." She shoved the little gift packet inside my coat pocket, and I promised to call her again soon for a catch up. It had stopped raining, and I got to the entrance to the car park just as Adam's BMW pulled in.

"Everything ok?" has asked as I fastened the seat belt and he pulled off.

"Yes thanks. You were right, we did have quite a chat about, you know - stuff."

"Good. And was she freaked out?"

"Surprisingly, no." I said, slipping my hand onto his thigh and giving it a squeeze. "Thank you."

18

We put the shopping away between us, then had crusty bread with cheese for lunch. After clearing the dishes away, I made a pot of tea, and Adam produced a box of chocolate coated Florentines to go with it. We moved to the sofa, and he flicked through the Sky channels to find a film.

"You know, all this lazing around and eating isn't good. We'll both get fat." I said, with a mouthful of the sweet nutty biscuit.

"Listen, it takes a lot of calories to maintain this manly physique" he stroked his stomach, lifting the bit of belly that protruded slightly over the waistband of his jeans. "And you've never complained about the awning over the toy shop." I snorted with laughter, almost spitting my drink out. "What, don't tell me you've never heard that expression?"

All I could do was shake my head, until eventually I regained enough composure to swallow the mouthful of tea. "No, I haven't. But you're right, you'll get no complaints from me. I never did go for skinny fellas. Besides, it goes with my muffin top."

We watched telly for most of the afternoon and chatted a bit more about the holiday. Then Adam made his apparently famous 'Spag Bol' for dinner, with garlic bread and salad, and we shared a bottle of red wine. To be fair, it was bloody good.

"Fancy a drive out somewhere tomorrow? Maybe have some lunch?" he asked. We'd moved back to the sofa and were listening to music while we finished the last of the wine. "I thought we could head over to Buxton maybe. It's a nice run, and the Grove Hotel does a decent Sunday lunch, then we could come back via Matlock Bath? Or if it's dry, we could go to Bakewell; have lunch at the Rutland, then a walk along the river?"

"Sounds lovely. I've never eaten an either, so you choose." I drained the last of my wine, put the glass on the coffee table, then stretched out, my head in his lap. "You're the boss."

Adam stroked my hair, and I closed my eyes, totally relaxed. Soon his hand moved down across my collar bone and snaked inside the top of my shirt. His fingers brushed lightly over the cup of bra, and my nipple instantly puckered under his touch. He slowly unfastened the buttons, one by one, then moved the material to the sides. He cupped my breast more firmly now, and I sighed. He began to knead my breasts, pinching and twisting my nipples until they both ached, hard as bullets, jutting through the thin lace fabric.

"Oh, God." I moaned, my eyes still closed.

"Nope. Just me." I heard the smile in his voice. "Now, are you going to be a good girl for me tonight?" His hand moved up to caress my cheek, and he dragged is thumb across my bottom lip. I opened my mouth, wanting to taste him, but his hand moved down to my neck. His fingers wrapped around my throat and squeezed gently, and I held my breath. He wasn't squeezing hard – just enough that I felt like I couldn't swallow, and I could hear my heart pounding in my ears. He let go and I gasped, my breathing hard and ragged, and I was aware of a sudden dampness between my legs. Adam let out a low chuckle.

"That really turns you on, doesn't it?" his hand moved back to my chest, and he slid his hand inside the cup of my bra, pushing the lace out of the way and lifting my breast free. "Get undressed" he said suddenly a few minutes later.

I sat up, and took of my shirt and bra, but then when I stood to unbutton my jeans, I hesitated, suddenly aware that I hadn't properly washed myself since the shower the night before.

"Wait, lets go upstairs. I need a shower." I bent to pick up my shirt, but he took hold of my wrist.

"I'll decide what you need. Now, don't make me ask again."

Reluctantly I did as I was told, though still protesting. "I feel all sweaty – I've had jeans on all day. Can I just go and wash quickly?" I stepped out of my jeans and pants, and he pulled me to stand in front of him. He was sitting forward on the sofa now, and closed his mouth around my nipple, while his hand dipped between my thighs.

"God you're wet!" he slid his fingers over my folds, making me blush. "And bodies all smell – it's natural. I'd rather smell your hot pussy than soap and perfume any day." As he spoke, he thrust two fingers inside me, and I let out a moan.

He unfastened his jeans, and shuffled them down, freeing his cock, before laying back on the sofa and pulling me onto his lap. I straddled him, moving my hips back and forth against his erection. We kissed, as he held me tightly, pressing my chest against his, then I sat up and his hands moved to my breasts.

"Lift up." He reached down between us to guide his cock into my entrance, and I groaned as I lowered myself down, sinking onto his length. I began to rock my hips, slowly, enjoying the feeling of having Adam inside me. His lay with his head back, his eyes half closed, enjoying my slow rhythmic movement. His hands rested gently on my hips, then moved to skim up my sides and over my breasts, his thumbs brushing over my nipples. He pinched them and smiled as he felt my inner muscles contract against his cock. He licked his lips and fixed me with such an intent stare, as he tweaked and pulled at the sensitive points, then held my hips as he began to move against me, circling his hips to match my rhythm.

I leaned forward now, clinging to the back of the sofa. Our mouths collided in an intense kiss – he bit and sucked as if he couldn't get enough of me, until I was gasping for breath. Leaning forward, my pelvis grinding against him, added friction against my clit, and I was soon climbing towards an orgasm.

"That's it. Good girl." I was panting hard now, and I screwed my eyes shut tight, trying to hold on to the feeling, hovering on the edge for just a few seconds longer before falling over the edge of control. I collapsed against Adam's chest as, whimpering, and he continued to rock his hips gently, while I rode out my orgasm.

His hands gripped my upper arms now, and he raised me up to sitting once again, as he gave me the most lascivious grin.

"Please... I can't..." I needed a minute to recover, but Adam had other ideas. He gripped my hips, lifting me as he began to thrust below me. The tempo increased, and he was slamming upwards into my pussy. I could hear the slapping of skin and the wetness of my arousal, as I braced my palms against his chest. He grunted with every thrust, and I leaned back, so I could feel every movement against my g-spot. His fingertips dug into my hips hard enough to leave bruises, then he let out a deep moan as he emptied his balls inside me. He slipped one hand down to where our bodies met, and pinched my clit, immediately sending me over the edge again. I cried out, my pussy contracting around him, milking every drop from his twitching cock, until his fingers relaxed their grip on my waist, and I collapsed against him in a sticky, sweaty heap. We were both clammy with sweat, and he moved the hair that clung to my forehead in damp tendrils.

"I can't get enough of you" he said, planting a kiss on my forehead. "What am I going to do with myself while you're away next weekend?"

"Well don't get any ideas about sending me filthy texts or video calling. I'll be sharing a bed with Ange, and I'll probably be far too drunk to be discreet."

"Is that right? Is she as sexy as you?"

"Behave!" I climbed off his lap, and looked around for my discarded clothes.

"Oh come on, a fella can dream." We headed upstairs towards. "Two posh young girls in a private boarding school? Barely legal, with raging hormones and no boys allowed on the premises? That's the stuff of most guys' fantasies."

While Adam put some laundry away, I used the loo and cleaned my teeth before stepping into the shower. He came in and leaned against the counter top, watching me while I soaped my body.

"I bet you girls used to shower together too after hockey, or lacrosse, or whatever it is they play at posh schools." I was about to say that we did no such thing, but the look on his face made it clear he was only teasing, and my denial would probably only have encouraged him.

"Actually, I never played hockey or lacrosse. I always hated games. We used to pretend to go cross-country running. We'd jog through the woods until we were out of sight, then we'd hop over the wall to the local petrol station, buy some cigarettes, and sit in the woods smoking for an hour. Then we'd rub a bit of mud on our legs and jog back, suitably out of breath. I'm sure the House Master was wise to it, but no-one ever said anything. They knew that most of the sixth formers drank and smoked, but as long as we were discreet, they stayed away from the known smoking haunts and left us to it."

"So were you parents loaded then?" Adam was in the shower now, while I dried myself off.

"Not at all. Dad worked in Dubai for a while, and you had to pay for school out there anyway, so the Company paid for it – whether it was local, or at back at boarding school in the UK, the costs were similar. I didn't get on with my parents at the time, and I wanted to go to carry on with my music, so chose to come back to here. I'd never really fitted in at school – we moved such a lot while I was growing up. Being there was so different. We were all thrown together sometimes thousands of miles away from any family. A lot of the kids had parents working overseas, whether in the forces or in business, and there were quite a few foreign students who had been sent to England to be educated. You were together seven days a week, so your housemates sort of became a surrogate family. I loved it there. Then towards the end of my first year, at the end of Lower Sixth, Dad lost his job. That meant they couldn't pay the school fees."

"That's shit. What happened?" he asked, climbing into the bed beside me.

"One of the teachers found out, and persuaded the school to help. They agreed it would be detrimental to my education to have to move to a different college half-way through a two-year course, so based on my 'outstanding contribution to the music department' and to school life in general, they gave me a full bursary for the second year, so I could finish my A Levels. As well as all the music stuff I did, I was a Cadet Sergeant in the RAF section, was doing my D of E Silver, was on the 'Ten Tors' team, and even volunteered as a chaperone for the third year girls summer camp during the holidays. I loved the whole boarding school life, and didn't really want to leave. I suppose it showed."

"Wow. So, not only a posh bird, but brainy, musically gifted, and a bit of a swat too, eh? What are you doing in Stoke with a fella like me?"

"Oh, I dunno. Perhaps I fancied a bit of rough."

Adam wrapped his arm around me, and I snuggled against his neck. "Well, I'm glad you did." He squeezed me in a tight hug, and I raised my head to meet his lips for goodnight kiss, before he reached over and turned off the bedside lamp.

Several minutes passed before he spoke quietly in the dark.

"But you do know, while you're away next week, I'll be wanking over the mental image of you two posh birds, drunkenly stumbling back to your hotel together and getting it on, don't you?" I tutted loudly, and he chuckled in the dark - although not completely sure whether he was joking.

19

On Sunday Adam decided we should drive over to Buxton for lunch. It was a grey morning, but the forecast promised some brightness in the afternoon, and the drive over the edge of the Peak National Park would be spectacular, even on a gloomy day. Somehow the dark skies and low cloud added to the atmosphere, conjuring up images of cloaked heroines fleeing across the heathland, like a scene from a Bronte or Du Maurier novel.

"You know, we really do live in a beautiful part of the world." I stared out of the window, watching as a ray of light shone through the parting clouds, and lit up the rock formations of The Roaches. "I mean we're not much more than an hour or so from either Manchester or Birmingham, and yet we're only 20 minutes from peace and quiet, and some of the most amazing scenery. We should get out and about more often."

"Yeah, we should. I often come out this way on the bike in the summer. The main routes like the Cat & Fiddle get quite busy, but there are plenty of great rides with sweeping bends and spectacular views. Or we could head over the Welsh Borders, do Snake Pass and the like. We'll have to get you kitted out." The look I gave him obviously conveyed my thoughts on the idea. "It's ok, I don't ride like I used to. I'm

Mr Slow-and-Steady these days - just happy to bimble along for a couple of hours and enjoy the scenery. If that includes stopping for bacon butty or a pie and a pint somewhere, even better."

We drove over the higher moors at Flash, before dropping down into Buxton a little after noon. Adam parked on the outskirts of the town, and we meandered slowly, stopping to browse in shop windows along the way. The Grove Hotel was hardly noticeable from the street. The shops of Grove Crescent formed part of a four-storey Victorian building. The frontages were all sheltered by the original cast iron and glass canopy. A large antique shop stood on the corner, double fronted, with expansive curved glass windows on either side of a central doorway, flanked by a pair neatly clipped standard bay trees in wrought iron planters. But it wasn't the door to the shop, it was the entrance to the hotel, which occupied the space on the three floors above the row of shop fronts. Inside the small porch was a menu board, and the inner door was open, to reveal a beautiful Victorian hallway with a wide sweeping staircase, ornately carved from glossy mahogany. At the top of the stairs the space opened out to a reception area, which was again furnished with dark polished wood.   The wallpaper was covered in exotic birds in shades of dark greens and teal blues, with accents of gold, which were picked up by the gleaming brass light fittings with Tiffany style shades or coloured glass.

The restaurant was a good deal brighter in its décor. The huge windows allowed the watery sunlight to stream in and offered stunning views across the tops of low stone cottages on the edge of the town and to the valley beyond. The Victorian paneling had been painted in a soft sage green, and the William Morris wallpaper had similar shades of muted grey/green foliage, with touches of mustard and pale yellow. The highbacked chairs were upholstered in a dull gold damask fabric, and there were crisp white cotton tablecloths which draped almost to the floor. We chose from the Table d'Hote lunch menu, and although the food was good, it wasn't remarkable. It was all well-cooked, well presented, and there was plenty of it – it was just a bit ordinary. However, the atmosphere and service made up for it. The whole experience felt like stepping back in time, as the waiters in tailored uniforms floated in and out of the tables, filling cut crystal glasses and delivering food on white bone china delicately edged in gold. The etiquette seemed almost Victorian too, and our waiter bowed slightly every time his asked if "Sir needed anything further" – always addressing Adam in the third person, and barely acknowledging me with more than a polite tight-lipped smile.

"You only come here because they treat you like a Dom." I commented, as soon as our waiter was out of earshot. "I bet you love it that they expect me to sit here quietly, and behave like a good little submissive, while you order my food and wine."

"Actually, I've only ever eaten here with clients or once with my mother, or I've had a drink in the bar when we've been to gigs at the Opera House. Although yes, now you mention it, it does amuse me." He smiled as he sipped his coffee and passed me both the chocolate mint thins. "Does it really bother you? I mean it's really nothing more than good old-fashioned chivalry. I've told you, I like taking care of you, even if that is ordering the food and wine. It's not meant to offend you – just make your life easier."

"No, it doesn't offend me. If it did, I would have made a point of speaking up to that waiter. In fact, I quite like being taken care of. I suppose that's why I liked public school. That was all quite old fashioned, with boys only being known by their surnames, and having to wear a blazer or a suit all the time, and the school Masters dressed in their black gowns. I liked knowing what the rules were, and everyone having to stick to them. Those that didn't like the discipline and pushed back didn't do very well. I enjoyed knowing exactly what was expected of me, and having my whole life timetabled and regimented.

What with lessons on a Saturday morning, and Chapel on a Sunday, we had very little time to think for ourselves, or to get into any real mischief I suppose."

"And that, my dear, is why you are so very good at doing as you're told, and will make an excellent sub." He stood, moving round to pull my chair out for me.

"What do you mean, *will make*?" I feigned indignation, and pouted as we walked back towards the reception desk and the stairs beyond.

"You know very well what I mean. This is a learning process for both of us, and it will take a while to settle into. And stop sticking your bottom lip out. I don't know whether to give in to the urge to bite it right now, or to give you a spanking later."

I blushed, quickly glancing around to make sure no-one had heard, then smiled at the thought.

20

We took the long way home. The sun was shining now, so we followed the minor roads through tiny villages and hamlets, winding our way back along the edge of Rudyard Lake, before heading back towards the city.

"Actually, when we get back to yours, I should probably head off. I need to sort some stuff out if I'm going away on Friday, and at least have an idea of what I'm going to take. I don't really want to be ironing and packing a bag at the last minute on Thursday night. Would you mind?"

"Course not. Besides I owe you a spanking, and you'd better get going, or who knows where that could lead. You might not be able to escape for hours."

When we got back to his house, Adam went straight through to the kitchen and filled the kettle. "You've got time for a cuppa, surely? You make the tea; I've got something for you." He flicked the kettle on, then disappeared upstairs. A few moments later, he came back down with a little grey drawstring pouch and held it out to me.

"What's this?" I said, taking it from him, and loosening the strings.

"Just a little something to remind you of me while you're away next weekend."

I took out two small silver-coloured objects. They were flat metal rings with a lacy filigree pattern, almost doughnut shaped, but instead of going all the way around in a circle, there was a gap – a bit like a C shape. They were slightly domed in the centre, and about the size of ten pence coin. I looked at him, not sure what I was to do with them. They seemed like jewellery, but certainly weren't like any kind of earrings I'd seen before.

"They're nipple cuffs." He said, reading the confusion on my face. "Here, you put each one around your nipple, and then pinch it to close the gap, so it's tight. They should be just tight enough so you know they are there, and your nipples stay hard and super sensitive, but no-one will know you're wearing them. That is unless of course you get undressed in front of someone." He wiggled his eyebrows suggestively, then popped them back into the pouch. "I want you to wear them all the time you're away. Facetime me, or send a picture wearing them before you leave on Friday, to give me something to look forward to when you get back."

"OK, but I imagine they'll get uncomfortable. I'm not sure I'll manage to keep them on all weekend." I slipped the pouch into my handbag.

"Oh yes you will, or there'll be consequences." He looked at me with scowl. "I might check in on you from time to time, just to make sure. And one more thing? You don't get to cum between now and next Sunday. In fact, you don't get to touch yourself at all, no matter how horny you get. No fingers, no vibrators, no leaning against the washing machine for the last spin cycle – nothing."

I was about to object, but he silenced me with his mouth on mine, before pinching my nipple hard enough to make me yelp.

"*Mwah ha hah!*" He mimicked an evil laugh, wringing his hands together, then picked up his tea and settled on the sofa, while I went to grab my things from the bedroom.

21

I arranged to have the Friday off work, and booked my train ticket. It was going to take half a day to get there with just one change at Bristol Temple Meads. Adam wanted to take me to the station on Friday morning, but I eventually convinced him I'd rather take a taxi, on the understanding that he could meet me from the train on Sunday afternoon. We met on Wednesday, just for a quick bite to eat after work, but by 8:30 we had headed to our respective homes. He reminded me again that I wasn't allowed to pleasure myself, and that he wanted photographic evidence to show how pretty my nipples looked when wearing my new jewellery.

I'd tried them on as soon as I got home that weekend, and it had taken a couple of attempts to get them tight enough to stay on, without cutting off the circulation completely. On Friday morning, I sent Adam a photograph first without a bra, then a second one so he could see them through the pink lace underwear. At first, I imagined everyone could see them, or somehow tell what I was wearing underneath my sweater and coat, which of course wasn't the case. Having got over the initial paranoia, I started to enjoy the feeling that I was up to something naughty, and settled back into my seat feeling rather smug.

The Royal Crescent Hotel was just a short taxi ride from the station. Angie had texted me to say she'd already arrived, and I should meet her in the Montague Bar, and I couldn't wait to see her. She was sat a table just inside, and jumped up to give me a tight hug, pressing herself against me. I squeezed her back, while my nipples throbbed at the contact. Adam had been right – they certainly were extremely sensitive.

Although we talked on the phone or by email regularly, Ange and I hadn't seen each other for almost four years, so had a good catchup over a couple of glasses of Prosecco. She didn't mention Mark, and I decided to wait for her to bring up the subject. We hadn't even checked in yet, so went to the front desk to collect our room keys, then took the lift up to the second floor. The room was beautifully furnished, classically elegant with a modern twist. In the centre was a huge four poster bed.

"Well, it *was* supposed to be romantic getaway. Oh well. Do you want me to see if they can move us to a twin?"

"Well, I doubt we'd get as good a view" I said, moving over to look out over the sweeping lawns to the front of The Crescent. "It's a gorgeous room, and I don't mind if you don't."

"Brill." Angie said and flopped on to the centre of the bed. "Oh god, this is so comfy!"

We decided to head into the town centre to do a bit of sightseeing, so I quickly messaged Adam to tell him that the hotel was gorgeous, and that were heading out for the afternoon. The city centre was only a ten-minute walk from the hotel, and the regency architecture was just beautiful. We went to the Jane Austen Centre, and enjoyed tea and scones with jam and clotted cream in the Regency Tea Rooms. Ange had always been a massive fan when we were at school, and one year for Christmas I'd bought her a beautifully leather-bound, if well-thumbed, edition of 'Pride and Predj' as she called it. She'd been a hopeless romantic in those days, and had dreamed of finding her own Mr Darcy. We made our way through the Artisan Quarter, and found a vibrant, eclectic mix of independent shops, selling everything from designer homewares to vintage clothing, and it was after six when we got back to the hotel.

When we arrived back at our room, there was a thick cream coloured envelope on the coffee table, with my name neatly hand-written on the front. I threw Ange a puzzled look, before opening it to read the contents. Inside was a gift voucher for £200 to be used in the hotel spa, and there was a typed note which simply said "Enjoy!" and underneath, the name Adam Taylor.

"Wow" exclaimed Ange. "That's so generous. To be honest, when I booked the room, the rate does include use of the pool, sauna and steam rooms, but the treatments aren't cheap. I was thinking we'd just chill in the spa for the afternoon, without booking anything that cost money. Now you can really treat yourself."

"Nonsense, we'll see what we can book for both of us to enjoy. You've already forked out the hotel, so it's only fair we share it. Grab that spa menu from the table, and we'll ring down to see what availability they have." The treatments were a bit pricey, but only what you'd expect. We booked a 'couples' aromatherapy massage for 11:00, followed by a cleansing facial at 1:30, giving us time to relax in the spa area in between, and knowing it would give us plenty of time to get dressed up and head out for the evening.

Ange had a shower, then when the bathroom was free, I went to run a quick bath and undressed while the water was running. I took off my bra and the heat in my nipples took me by surprise. While contained in my underwear they had felt sensitive – almost like sunburn, but as soon as they were set free there was a delicious tightness and throbbing, and they ached to be touched. I wasn't sure whether I should remove them to shower, or whether if I took them off, I'd be able to get them back on again. Instead, I took a couple of pictures on my phone in front of the mirror to send to Adam. Then, feeling really naughty as I washed myself, I decided to take some more shots in the bath. I worked up a creamy lather with some bodywash, and filmed myself with soap suds running down between my breasts and over my aching nipples, then quickly sent it to Adam.

When I came out of the bathroom, Ange was lazing on the bed, still in her towel, and asked "Do we have to go out? I'm not sure I can be bothered."

"Course not" I replied. "It's been a long day – I'm happy to stay here. Are you hungry?"

"Not really, after the size of that scone. We could always go down to the bar for a nightcap and see if we can get some nuts or crisps. What do you reckon?"

"Sounds good to me." I replied, brushing my hair through. She pulled on jeans and a sweater while I tied my hair into a loose bun, and we headed down to the hotel bar.

I had just ordered us a bottle of prosecco, when my phone buzzed. It was Adam.

> Nice - tho u really should warn if NSFW.
>
> Was in a room full of people. Naughty girl ;)

Angie saw me blush. "Adam, I take it? Oh god, he isn't sending you filthy texts is he?" she laughed.

"Sort of. I sent him a picture." I bit my lip. We'd never had any secrets and shared everything - even boys - back in our school days.

"Zoe Finch, I never thought you had it in you! I suppose I should be offended that you're sexting your fella while we're supposed to be having a girls only weekend, but I can't blame you. So, what did he say?"

"Nothing really, except that I'm very, very naughty." I giggled sheepishly.

"Ooh, did he threaten to put you over his knee when you get home?" I said nothing, but blushed furiously again. "Oh my god, he did, didn't he? You kinky so-and-so!"

"Don't say it like that – there's nothing wrong with having a bit of harmless fun." I had told Ange about Adam not long after we'd met, but there were aspects of the relationship that I wasn't ready to share just yet.

"Hey, listen, I'm all for it. I used to beg Mark to spice things up a bit, but he thought it was all a bit weird, and he was downright horrified when I tried to get him to watch some BDSM porn."

"You mean you're into all that stuff then?" I asked, shocked by her frankness.

"Not really, I mean I don't know. He wasn't willing to try anything. I did suggest a bit of spanking or light bondage, and even got some of those furry handcuffs – I was going to bring them with me this weekend. I've read some erotica for women, and bits of it really turned me on, but only quite tame stuff. I'd probably run a mile if someone actually tried to tie me up."

"I take it there's definitely no way back for you two then?" I asked, suddenly sad for my friend.

"No. But don't worry, I'm not going to get all depressed. We've both tried our best, but we just aren't the same people that met all those years ago. We want different things now. It just felt so... stale, I suppose. He always thought that eventually I'd want to settle down and have kids, but there's so much more I want to do with my life. I was just so bored with the whole routine... drinks with work friends on a Friday, out for a meal together on a Saturday, lunch with his parents alternate Sundays. And they never stopped banging on about wanting grandkids, and my ticking biological clock!" She sighed, and drained her glass, before topping us both up.

"And what about work?" I asked. "Is that a bit weird, or don't you really see each other in the day?"

"No not really, but it was getting a bit difficult. Quite a few of our mutual friends are couples, and people had stopped coming out socially, because they didn't want to take sides. You know David, my boss? Well, he's getting married in July, to one of Mark's colleagues, Anthony, from Legal. It was going to be super awkward to both go to the wedding, especially if we were to each going to turn up with someone else. So anway, I gave my notice when we went back after Christmas. I've got two weeks until I finish."

"What? Oh Ange, you didn't. What are you going to do now? I mean, if you've already agreed Mark can have the house and buy you out, you'll still need a job to be able to buy somewhere yourself, or even to rent."

"I know. I'll find something else pretty quickly, I'm sure. I've started putting my CV out with a couple of recruitment firms in the area, and Mel says I can crash with her for as long as I need to."

That wasn't going to be ideal. Ange's sister Melina was a bit of an 'earth mother' type. She had three kids and two dogs, was active on the PTA, did lots of crafting, and was married to a tree surgeon, who brewed his own wine. They were a lovely family – in small doses – but it certainly wasn't going to be easy for anything more than a stop-gap.

"Come and stay with me." I blurted out, after returning from the loo.

"Yeah, right. Ask me again when you're not pissed."

"No, I'm serious. And I'm not pissed" I smiled, after nearly knocking my glass off the edge of the table. "Well, maybe just a bit squiffy, but at least think about it. I've got a spare room, and they say Stoke's fast becoming the call centre capital of the UK. There must be loads of jobs going for someone with your experience."

"It's a lovely offer, but don't you think you'd better have a chat with Adam before you start inviting me to play gooseberry?"

"Why? He was his own place, and I stay there from Friday to Sunday. We don't often do much in the week, because he works late. You'd have the place to yourself all weekend, and I wouldn't charge you any rent, just sort your own food, and give me a couple of quid towards the bills if you can, but we can work all that out. Just at least think about it?"

"Ok, ok, I'll think about it. But anyway, this bottle's empty, so that must mean it's time for bed. Come on." And with that she stood, holding out her had to pull me up.

22

The breakfast was amazing. We filled up, knowing that we could skip lunch then eat out later that evening. We had granola and fruit compote, then I had the eggs benedict, while Ange ordered the avocado on toast, topped with a poached egg and streaky bacon. There didn't seem any hurry for us to leave the restaurant, so we ordered a second pot of coffee, and picked at a couple warm pastries, then finished with some fresh strawberries.

"God, I'm stuffed" I sat back, downing the last bit of my freshly squeezed orange juice. "I dread to think how huge my belly is going to look in a swimming costume later."

"Nonsense, you've got an amazing figure. I wish I had your curves. I've got no more bust now than I had when I was 12, and absolutely no arse!"

"What? I wish I could eat like you do and not put weight on. I bet you still weigh the same as you did at school. When I met you that first term, I thought you must be so sporty – you looked so athletic." Ange had always been stick-thin, despite eating like a horse.

"Ha! I don't think our cross country could ever be called sport. Fuck knows how we ever got away without Botch finding out." I laughed at the memory. The girls games teacher was of Italian descent, and called Miss Borelli, otherwise known as Bottichelli, or just 'Botch'.

"I don't think she could give a shit. We were discreet, so she stayed out of our way" I reasoned. "The ones that hung around Main School, where they could be a bad influence on the third form were the only ones that got nicked. Come on."

We went back to the room to chill before getting ready for our first treatment. I'd removed the nipple cuffs when I went to bed, and luckily, the two bottles of prosecco numbed any pain that I would otherwise have felt. I was suddenly aware that not only had I forgotten to put them back on, but I didn't know whether I was supposed to keep them on while we were in the Spa. There was no way I could contemplate lying with my weight on them while having a massage, and they would be obvious to anyone who saw me in a swimsuit. I decided to call Adam, so told Ange I'd catch her up.

"Hey sexy" he answered straight away. "I didn't expect to hear from you. Having a good time?"

"Yeah, brill thanks, I can't wait to tell you all about it. Listen, I just wanted to ask you something. You know you said I have to keep these nipple things on all weekend, well is it ok if I don't wear them in the spa today? I'm having a massage, and then we'll be in and out of the pool, and it's just going to be really uncomfortable."

"I didn't expect you to keep them on in the spa to be honest, so thank you for asking me, but yes, you have my permission to remove them for a short while. You can put them on again when you get dressed and send me another picture. Are you out tonight?"

"Yes, we're going into town. We found a Mexican place we liked the look of, and they have live music at the weekends, so we'll check that out."

"Good. Just imagine how much they're going to throb when you're shaking your funky stuff after a few tequilas. And every time another bloke stares at those fantastic tits, you can imagine me pinching them and claiming what's mine."

"Fuck, Adam, why do you do that?" I asked, my voice thick with desire.

"Because you fucking love it. It makes you wet, you little slut. Now, don't forget, no touching. You'll get what you deserve tomorrow. See you then, sexy." The call ended, and I followed Ange and headed up to our room to get changed.

23

The spa was wonderful. The staff were extremely attentive, and after a short tour of the facilities, we had a quick dip in the hydrotherapy pool, then were offered refreshments and relaxed on one of the heated stone beds, until we were escorted to the massage suite. We had booked a couples massage, so were side by side in the same room, each having the same treatment. We were offered a selection of different aromatherapy oils, with a brief description of their properties, and opted for an uplifting blend of ylang-ylang and neroli.

It felt a little weird being naked beside my old friend, but I soon relaxed and enjoyed the amazing massage, as heated stones were smoothed over my oiled skin, from the soles of my feet up to my back and neck, then along my arms to my fingertips. After turning over, my masseuse concentrated on my neck and shoulders, while seated at the top of my head. Her fingers pinched and pressed at various points across my forehead and face, and along my jaw line, finally lacing her hands under my chin and across my neck.

She then applied a cooling cleanser across my face and neck area, then followed with a gel-like serum which she smoothed on my forehead and eye area before covering my face with a cool damp muslin cloth. A lay for a few minutes enjoying the wonderful tingling sensation, then once again, she cleansed my skin with cotton pads, which were soaked in something with a clean fresh scent, leaving my skin feeling revitalized. We were instructed to relax, and to take our time getting up slowly, and to make sure we rehydrated properly.

We went from there to the "experience shower" and walked through different stages including green-lit tropical downpour, through a hot shower with warming red lights and steaming body jets, then cooled as we walked under a waterfall, ending with a tepid mist that was so fine it was like being in a cool cloud of blue light.

After enjoying a glass of sparking fruit spritz in the hot tub, we relaxed on the hot stone benches again. The room was in semi darkness, the ceiling lit with pin pricks of light to resemble a starry sky, and we both nodded off.

Later that afternoon, we went back to the room and had a cup of tea, while we took our time getting ready to go out. Ange was almost as tall as me, but slim to the point of being almost too thin. She was wearing a short skirt of deep burgundy leather, with dark tights of the same colour, and black suede boots to the knee. She wore billowing semi-sheer blouse with a paisley pattern in muted shades of deep reds and black with tiny accents of gold, pulled in at the waist with a thin gold belt, and finally a black suede biker-style jacket. Her dark hair was normally in a neat bob, but now looked mussed up and sexy. Her eyes were rimmed in dark kohl liner, and she wore a vivid red lipstick.

I wore skinny black velvet trousers, a grey and purple silk tunic, and my favourite four-inch heeled boots in a pewter-coloured snake-effect leather. I was wearing the new nipple jewellery, as per Adam's instructions, and was careful that my sculpted bra had just enough padding to hide my achingly erect nipples. I curled my hair, and pinned it up in a loosely, adding smokey dark purple eye shadow with just a touch of sparkle, and long drop earrings with grey pearl beads. It was cold out, so I carried a purple cashmere pashmina, which I could wrap around my shoulders during the short walk into town.

"Wow, check us two hotties!" Ange exclaimed, as we stood side by side looking in the full-length mirror before we left the room. We walked arm in arm across the hotel lobby, and giggled liked school-girls when a group of men turned and very obviously checked us out as we walked by.

We went back to what was called the Artisan Quarter, where there seemed to be lots of bars and restaurants, and the streets were busy with groups of young people and couples enjoying the atmosphere. We found the Mexican restaurant that we had spotted earlier in the day, and although it was still quite early, most of the tables were full. We were shown up to the first floor where there were more dining tables on a kind of mezzanine which ran across the large space, looking down over the small dance floor.

We had several dishes and shared them, starting with crisp tortilla chips loaded with chilli, cheese and jalapenos, then pulled pork fajitas, halloumi and vegetable skewers, and seabass with pineapple salsa, and fried baby potatoes in hot habanero sauce. We drank ice cold Sol beer served with lime wedges. Ange then persuaded me to try the tequila shots which arrived on a wooden paddle, and accompanied by card with tasting notes to describe the three different shots. First was the sharp citrus and agave Blanco, which to be honest, took my breath away – and not in a good way. Second was the honey coloured Reposado, which had a slightly sweeter flavour with hints of vanilla, and finally the Anejo, aged for three years, which had the darkest colour of all and a smoothness which made it more palatable, although I wasn't sure whether I could actually say I enjoyed any of them.

Several beers later, we were jostling for space on the tiny dancefloor, and shouting along to the chorus of every song, whether we actually knew the lyrics or not. It was just after midnight when I finally dragged Ange away.

"No, *not* just one more." I implored, handing her the suede jacket that I had retrieved along with my shawl. "My feet are killing me!" They weren't the only thing throbbing right now and I couldn't wait to free myself from what now felt like instruments of torture.

"Serves you right for wearing fuck-me heels like that." She stuck her tongue out at me, while I pulled her towards the door. We stumbled back through the streets, still busy people despite the hour, and found our way back to the hotel.

"Nightcap?" she gestured towards the bar.

"Really? Aren't you tired?" She shook her head, grinning, and linked her arm through mine, steering me towards the bar. "Urgh - doesn't look like I have much choice." I ordered a cranberry juice and a bottle of water, while Ange had a double vodka and lime. "You're going to have such a hangover tomorrow" I warned.

24

I was right. Ange groaned, dragging the covers up over her head as I opened the heavy curtains to let the daylight into the room.

"Come on, or we'll miss breakfast." It was already 9:30, and we only had half an hour to before they stopped serving.

"Just leave me here to die" she wailed dramatically, but then added "Or at least make me a strong coffee."

I switched on the kettle, then passed her a bottle of water and a couple of paracetamol, while I dressed and began putting clothes back in my bag. Ange sat up on the edge of the bed and threw back the pills, wincing as she washed them down. Her eyeliner was smudged, and her hair stuck up on one side of her head.

"God, I'm too old for this." She pulled on a pair of leggings and a sweater. "I don't even remember what time we came up. Was I really pissed?"

"I think we both were, but at least I stopped drinking and switched to water. You had another two doubles in the bar when we got back. I'm surprised you aren't throwing up." I passed her the trainers she'd been wearing when we arrived.

"There's time yet" she replied, struggling to bend and fasten her shoes, so I pushed them onto her feet and tied the laces.

After a couple of strong coffees and a bowl of granola and fruit, Ange at least got some colour back, and said she was feeling better. Neither of us could face the full bacon and eggs, but did both have toasted English muffins with jam, and I took a banana for each of us as we went back to the room to pack.

After packing our bags and checking the bathroom and drawers for a final time, we went down to settle the bill for our drinks and food, and asked the Receptionist to call us a taxi to the station. There was an icy wind blowing as we stepped into the street, and I pulled my jacket around me, my nipples suddenly springing to attention under the thin sweater. They felt incredibly tender, and I hadn't been able to contemplate squeezing the rings around them for another day. Instead, I had dropped them into my purse, and told myself I'd put them back on in the train toilet before Adam met me later that afternoon.

"Well, bye lovely. I've had such a good time." Ange hugged me tightly as we stood in the station. "I don't know why we don't do this more often."

"Bye sweetheart. And thanks again for asking me." I took both of her hands in mine. "Call me soon. And I'm serious, if you want to come and stay, the offer still stands. Any time."

"I'll give it some thought – promise." She kissed me on the cheek, then picked up her bag and turned towards the stairs that led over the footbridge to the other platforms. "And enjoy your spanking!" she shouted over her shoulder, grinning.

I shook my head, laughing. A middle-aged couple standing a few feet away had obviously heard, judging from the look of abject horror on the woman's face. The man just raised his eyebrows, as I tossed my hair back and gave them a wide smile, before going taking a nearby seat on the platform to wait for my train.

25

After changing again at Bristol Temple Meads I tried to read, but I was nodding off, and was afraid I'd miss my station. At Birmingham New Street I bought a coffee and a limp tuna mayo sandwich, along with a bar of chocolate which I shoved into my bag to eat on the last leg of the journey. It was only going to take another 45 minutes to get to Stoke, so I thought I better put my 'jewellery' back on and went off to find the ladies toilet.

Safely inside a cubicle, I lifted up my sweater and dragged my bra straps down my shoulders as far as I could, then winced as I tried to attach the first ring. I gasped as I squeezed the thin metal to close it around my nipple, which felt as though it was on fire. The second was even harder, and I had to count to three and brace myself for the pain. I held my breath for a few seconds, my hands cupped over my breasts to take their weight and reduce the pressure. Thankfully, once in place, the pain eased enough that I could pull my bra back up and lower my sweater. A few minutes later my train pulled in, so I found my seat and settled back to eat my chocolate, acutely aware of the dull throbbing in my nipples which was amplified by every movement of the train as it swayed along.

Adam was waiting in the foyer of the station, and I waved to him as I walked through the barrier. He immediately walked over to meet me and planted a kiss on my lips before taking my bag with one hand and draping the other around my shoulder. I would never get tired of how small I felt tucked under his arm, and pressed myself against his side, my arm wrapped around his waist as we walked.

"Ooh, I've missed you.!" I said, squeezing him as we negotiated our way out through the doors and on to the pavement.

"I must admit, I've missed you too - even though it's only been an extra two days. It surprised me, actually. I must be getting used to having you around." He led me across the road to where he was parked, and put my bag in the boot, then pinned me against the side of the car for a proper greeting. One hand moved to the back of my neck, the other wrapped around my waist inside my coat and he pressed himself against me, kissing me long and hard, and triggering the sharp pain in my nipples once again. "My place, or do you want to eat first?" he asked, as he released his grip.

"Can we go to my place, for a change?" I asked. "I could do with sorting some washing. Although I don't think I've got much to eat."

"Who needs food? That's the last thing on my mind." he wiggled his eyebrows for comic effect, and we got into the car. It was only a short drive to the village where I lived, and I told him about the hotel room, the spa, the food, and of course Ange getting drunk on tequila and vodka.

"She was pretty rough this morning, although I think she felt better after breakfast. I was worried about her feeling ok on the way back, but she's not got so far to go, and she already text me to say she's back home. Not that she will be able to call it that much longer."

"Is she going to have enough money to buy somewhere for herself?" asked Adam. "I mean you said there was quite a bit of equity in the house?"

"Well, she'll have a decent deposit alright, but she's packed her job in. She said it was just getting too awkward, both working for the same firm. She won't be able to get a mortgage until she's working so she's talking about staying with her sister until she finds something."

"It's a shame she doesn't want to move up to Stoke and work for you" he suggested. "Could she solve your staffing problems?"

"If only. I did suggest she'd be welcome to come and stay if she needs a break, but she's way over-qualified for our place. And I bet she earns about ten grand a year more than we'll be offering."

Having stopped off to grab milk and bread, Adam put the kettle on while I took my bag upstairs. I had just opened it to unpack, when he appeared in the bedroom doorway.

"So, are you going to show me?" he stood with his head on one side, clearly staring at my chest.

"If I must." I began to lift my sweater. "They're really uncomfortable; I can't wait to take them off." After pulling my sweater over my head, I slid my bra straps down. I drew in a sharp breath through my teeth as my breasts were suddenly free of their support, and the cool air hit my tender nipples.

"Fuck Zo, you look gorgeous. Come here." He stepped towards me.

"No, please, they're so sore!" I backed away, my hands covering my tits, but he took my wrists and moved them down by my sides. Then, sitting on the edge of the bed, he turned me to face him. I held my breath, as he flicked his tongue across my aching nipple. His touch was so light, but it felt like a lightening bolt, and I groaned at the exquisite combination of pleasure and pain. He lifted my breasts together, then licked them both, circling around the puckered skin in their tortuous silver collars.

When he removed them in turn, the pain made me cry out. The release of each constricting ring caused a sudden surge of blood flowing to the area making the over-sensitive bud throb. As he did so, he immediately took my nipple into his mouth, the heat of his tongue soothing and calming the enflamed skin, until my breathing slowed down to somewhere near normal. By the time he had taken them both off, I was whimpering with need, a fiery ache in my pussy.

I straddled Adam's lap as he still sat on the edge of the bed, and we kissed. It was tender at first, but grew more urgent, until I was pulling at his sweater, grinding against the bulge in his jeans. He tipped me off, and I stood to hurriedly undress. Within seconds we were both naked, and he threw me on to the bed, quickly positioning himself between my legs. He gripped my thigh, pushing it up over his back, before burying his length inside me with one deep thrust, crushing me against the bed.

Has was still for just a moment, then he withdrew, and again thrust hard and deep. His arms were under my shoulders, his full weight on top of me, and each thrust literally took my breath away, forcing the air from my lungs with a groan. After a few more minutes, he raised his weight up on his arms, and began moving his pelvis, faster and faster, grunting with each thrust. I raised both my legs over his shoulders, allowing him to go even deeper, digging my fingers into his buttocks as if to pull him into me, while he held my thighs hard enough to leave bruises.

"Sorry babe... Can't hold this one back... Aaarrgh!" he let out a guttural moan, and with gritted teeth and his eyes screwed tight shut, I felt the warmth of his seed empty inside me, as his cock pulsed. I clenched my inner muscles around him. "Ooh hoo, No!" He jumped as if in pain, then rolled onto his back beside me. We were both breathing hard, and a sheen of sweat covered our bodies.

"Blimey, you have missed me!" I smiled, turning to look at Adam. "You ok?" My fingers brushed his.

"Mm hmmm." His eyes were closed, and I watched as the rise and fall of his chest gradually slowed down. "Sorry, that wasn't quite the welcome home I'd planned."

"Hey, it's nice to know I can make Mr Control Freak lose it sometimes." I smiled. "You can make it up to me later."

"Ok, but I might need an hour to recover."

Five minutes later, Adam was asleep. When I woke him, he was full of apologies, but it was obvious that he was exhausted, having worked all day on Saturday. We went for a walk to the local shop, just picking up a couple of basics. I made a quick meal of pasta with pesto and sundried tomatoes from a jar, and a frozen garlic baguette, but then despite his protests, insisted he went home.

"But I owe you - I wanted to really show you how much I missed you this weekend. Besides, who's the Dom here?" he took a fistful of my hair, pulling my head back to claim my mouth.

"Forget it." I wriggled free. "New rule - I've decided you don't get to boss me around in my own house. I need a bath and an early night – alone!"

"Is that so? What if I don't want to obey your new rule. You're still wearing my collar, remember?" His arms were around me again, pulling me into his body. "I could just tie you up, then you'd be at my mercy."

"Listen *Sir*, as much as I'd love you to stay, you need some sleep." I could feel his erection pressing against my thigh. "I'm telling you now, if you're thinking of starting something, I *will* use my safeword." He scowled, and finally let me go.

"Hmmm, I'm not sure I like it when you get feisty. But you're right – I am fucking knackered."

"Then go home and go to bed. Give me a ring tomorrow night." I steered him towards the front door, then we kissed again, and he couldn't resist tweaking my sore nipple. "Will you just bloody well go!" I laughed.

"OK, sorry. I'll call you tomorrow. Night sexy"

"G'night Sir" I smiled sweetly, and he shook his head as he turned and left.

26

Work was manic on Monday morning, but I did manage to post advertisements for the vacancies. I didn't like using agencies, and being based in a fairly small town, we always managed to recruit through word of mouth, offering current employees a small incentive payment if they referred someone who complete the three-month probationary period. I put notices on our Company Intranet as well as sending a general email, and putting the vacancy details on the notice board in the staff kitchen area. A couple of people approached me on their breaks to say they knew someone who'd be interested and promised to get application forms or CVs back to me.

At the end of the day, I was just finishing up some queries, when Chris approached my desk and handed me his CV. I thanked him, and carried on typing.

"I was hoping you'd read through it, if you've got a few minutes" he said, pulling a chair over to sit in front of my desk. "I mean, you know I'm qualified. Or do you fancy going out for a drink, and we can discuss it."

"Sorry Chris, I really haven't got time right now. I'm going to block out some time later this week to go through any applications I get. I need to be fair – I hope understand."

"Yeah, yeah - course. I suppose you can't be seen to show any favouritism." I hoped that would be the end of it, but as he stood, he spoke again. "Erm, I did wonder if you'd like to go out for a drink sometime anyway, or maybe go for some food? You know, maybe next week sometime, if you're free."

"What, like a date?" I tried not to look horrified. "I'm flattered, honestly, but I've always made it a rule of mine not to get involved with work colleagues, sorry. It makes it difficult to carry on working together if you split up, and besides, can you imagine how awkward it would be to discipline someone who you're going out with?"

"Oh, I don't know, I wouldn't mind being disciplined by someone like you."

I tried to smile, and pretended I hadn't noticed his inference, but sat dumfounded as he left. Surely, he wasn't hoping I'd give him the job in exchange for a lasagna and a glass of wine at the local pub?

Adam called that evening, just as she'd finished eating. "Hey sweetheart. Did you get a decent night's sleep?"

"Yeah, I did. Sorry about last night. I was in bed by about half-nine, and slept right through. I feel better for it though. How was your day?" he asked. I decided not to mention Chris asking me out.

"Good thanks. I've put the job details about and had a couple of sniffs already."

"I bet that fella Chris is one of them. Have you decided whether to give him a chance?"

"I can't." I said emphatically. "He'd just create more problems that he'd solve. I'd end up losing staff, or at the very least, spending half my time refereeing battles. Hopefully someone else will come forward, and if not, I'll get some call takers in to fill the gaps, then perhaps put it out to an agency. I don't know."

"Probably a good idea. But you're still going to have to tell him straight when he doesn't get the job, and from what you've said, he isn't going to take it well."

"Yeah, I know. I'll cross that bridge when I come to it, but to be honest, if he really thinks he can do so much better, then good luck to him. I won't lose any sleep if he decides to go."

We chatted some more, and given that Adam was working late all week again, we confirmed that I'd see him on Friday. "Shall I come straight to yours? What time will you be back?"

"I've already told the Shift Manager he's got to be in an hour early on Friday, so I can be away on time. I lied and told him I've got an appointment. I think I give them enough unpaid overtime."

"Good for you. So, take away? Or would you like me to cook? What do you fancy?" I asked.

"Neither, we're going out. I'll pick you up at seven. And put a dress on." It wasn't a question.

"Yes Sir!" I answered, mockingly. "Where are we going?"

"Never you mind, and cut the sarcasm too. We're going out for dinner, and you will accompany me as my sub. That's all you need to know. Wear something sexy, with your hair up, and your collar on of course."

"Of course." I smiled to myself. I loved it when Adam was in his sexy Dom mode. "I'll look forward to it, Sir."

27

For the next couple of days, Chris was starting to push his luck. Whenever I went to get a coffee, or have a break, he seemed to be hanging around, or making excuses to come by my desk. And worse than that, he was trying to flirt with me, in a rather odd way.

"You're right, it wouldn't be a good idea for us to get together" he said out of the blue as I stood waiting for my lunch to ping in the microwave. "I mean, you look like you might be trouble in the bedroom. I bet you're a real handful." He blatantly looked me up and down as he said it.

"That's enough Chris. I really don't want to take this to HR, but there's a line you don't cross in the workplace, let alone with your boss. And quite frankly, if that's the sort of thing you say to women, it's no wonder you're single."

"What? It was meant as a compliment!" he looked genuinely stunned by my reaction, as if I should think he was a catch.

"I don't care how you meant it, just drop the subject. I've tried to be nice, but actually, I'm in a relationship, and to be brutally honest, you wouldn't get a look in even if I weren't." I threw the

uneaten lunch into the bin, and stormed back to my
desk.

Chris didn't speak to me for the rest of the day, but I
couldn't concentrate. I went from anger, and
wishing I'd slapped him across the face, to feeling
guilty, wondering whether I'd given him any signals
that could have been misread, or encouraged him in
some way.   I didn't really want to go down the
disciplinary route, because he'd probably lose his
job, and selfish as it sounded, I couldn't afford to lose
a top call taker. I needed a second opinion, and tried
to call Ange when I got home, but she was out
somewhere very noisy, obviously enjoying herself,
and I didn't want to spoil her evening, so said it
wasn't important.

Adam sent me a text just after nine, and asked if I'd
had a good day. I didn't feel like talking about it, so
my answer was a bit short, and he rang me
immediately.

"What's wrong babe? Bad day?" he asked, genuine
concern in his voice. I sighed before answering.

"You could say that. I had a bit of a run in with Chris.
He was a total dick today, and was trying to flirt with

me I think, so I put him in his place. I'll be fine after a decent night's sleep."

"You don't sound fine. What happened?" He waited, but I wasn't sure where to start.

"He asked me out the other day. I made up some crap about not dating in the workplace – you know, don't shit where you eat, and all that – but he's been a bit creepy, that's all."

"And you're telling me now?" I didn't expect him to be pleased, but I didn't expect Adam to get quite so angry. "When was this? Zoe, I want to know exactly what he's been saying."

"Oh please, if this is because you're jealous, don't be. Even if I wasn't with you, he's about five foot three and ginger. Give me some credit! I just can't get over why he would think he stood a chance, or that making creepy comments about me being "a handful" would get him anywhere. I keep thinking maybe I must have said or done something that he's misconstrued along the way."

I managed to calm Adam down, after playing down some of what Chris had said.

"Honestly, he probably just thought it was the best way to get my attention, and make sure he gets the job. He seemed genuinely surprised when I reacted and told him he'd crossed he line. I know it's no defence, but I don't think he meant to be offensive. He's so full of himself, he probably thought I'd be flattered!"

"Listen, it's your call, but creeps like that need dealing with. If not, they think that kind of behaviour is acceptable, and keep treating other women like that. The guy sounds like a moron."

"I know, I'll deal with it. Promise." I tried to change the subject. "Anyway, are you going to give me any more hints about where we're going on Friday night?"

"Nope. You'll find out soon enough."

"Aww, I hate secrets – I don't know what to wear!" I whined.

"Don't start. I've told you – all you have to do is look sexy. And sulking will only get you a spanking."

28

By Friday, things were at least a little bit quieter on the phones. It had been two weeks since Christmas, so all the usual calls about returning gift purchases, or getting rings re-sized, had started to finally die right down. I'd had a fair few application forms and CVs for roles in the call centre and picked out a handful to contact for interview the following week. There was no other interest in the more senior role, and although I still hadn't decided what the job title or specifics of the role would be, I had outlined the sort of person I was looking for to step up in my email to all the staff. I just knew I couldn't possibly offer it to Chris, regardless of his recent indiscretion, and was really hoping that Megan or Josie, one of the other more senior members of the team, would apply.

At five o'clock, I switched the phones over, and for a change, followed the rest of the staff out of the building. I was usually at least half an hour clearing my emails, but I was determined to lock up and get away on time, so I could shower and sort my hair out, and I still hadn't decided what to wear.

"Come on ladies, have you got no homes to go to?" I ushered out a group of three of the younger staff, who were stood around with their phones out, sharing the latest celebrity gossip. I followed them through the foyer, switching the lights off and setting the alarm, before locking the front door and heading to my car. Leaning against my car, looking gorgeous in an immaculately tailored blue suit, was Adam.

"Hey, sexy" he grinned, with that crooked smile that under any other circumstances, would go straight to my core.

"Hi, er … what are you doing here?" I asked, a little flustered. I realised that people who normally dashed off as soon as they could, were now loitering, chatting by their cars, or rifling through handbags under the pretence of lost keys, obviously dying to know who he was.

"Well, that's a nice welcome." He stood up, reaching to wrap one hand around the back of my neck, then leaned in for a long lingering kiss, which I broke off as quickly as I could. "I missed you today. And I wanted to make sure you put something sexy on, before I whisk you off for the evening."

People were staring, nudging each other, or giving me sideways glances. Chris glared at me from his car, which was parked next to mine, and shook his head before revving his engine loudly, and driving off. Adam's eyes followed him until he was through the gates, and it suddenly dawned on me that this had all been a show for his benefit.

"Well, thanks very much" I hissed "but I'm sure I can manage to dress myself." I ducked free of his arm, got into my own car and drove off, leaving Adam stood there, looking bewildered.

I was fuming. I was so angry that by the time I got home, I was fighting back tears. I took off my work clothes, and pulled on some old joggers and a sweater, then poured half a bottle of white wine into a huge glass and took a couple of enormous gulps. I sat on the bottom of the stairs, still trying to process what had just happened, and what to do about it. A few minutes later, there was a knock at the door.

"You've got to be kidding" I muttered to myself, but sure enough, Adam stood there as if nothing had happened.

"You're not getting ready, come on." Then saw the look on my face, before I turned my back on him, shaking my head in disbelief. "What's wrong baby?"

"For fucks sake, Adam. I can't believe you did that." I picked up the bottle of wine from the kitchen, topping up my already half-empty glass, and taking it through to the lounge.

"Did what? Came to surprise you after work? I thought you might be pleased to see me. Instead you're here knocking back wine, and sulking like a bloody kid. What's your problem?"

"*I'm* sulking? You've got some nerve!" I stared at him in disbelief. "That was never about surprising me, was it; it was about marking your territory. You belittled me in front of everybody, or should I say in front of Chris. For fucks sake - are you really that insecure?" I sat down on the sofa and took another swallow of wine. "Well at least you've given everyone something new to gossip about. Nice move!"

"Don't raise your voice at me, Zoe" he grabbed me by the wrist, taking the glass from my hand, and putting on the side table. "You need to control that temper of yours, and show some respect. Have you forgotten who's in charge here? You agreed to wear my collar, and you need to remember exactly what that entails."

"Oh no you don't!" I stood up and backed away from him, suddenly feeling as if he was invading my space. "You seem to have forgotten, but that only applies when I'm *actually wearing* your collar, which right now, I'm not. You may think you can control me at weekends because of it, but I never agreed for you to come to my workplace and embarrass me like that."

"So ok, it was a bonus to show that Chris fella – or I presume that's who was in the car that sped off. So what? You said yourself he crossed the line, and you weren't doing anything about it. I just didn't want him trying it on with you, thinking you'd made up some imaginary boyfriend just as an excuse to put him off. I don't know why you don't want anyone to know about us anyway. Don't you want me to meet your friends? Are you ashamed of us?"

"You don't get it do you? Those people are *not* my friends. They're colleagues, nothing more, and I am their boss." He still just looked genuinely surprised my reaction.

"Look, I don't believe in mixing business with pleasure, and I've always been careful to share very few details of my life with those I work with. Just enough to be polite, without giving anything away. What we have – our relationship – it's personal. Private."

He pressed his fingertips to his temples and closed his eyes, as if trying to ward off a stress headache, then spoke again more calmly. "Ok, it was a selfish of me, and maybe I over-reacted about Chris, but you have no idea how much it pisses me off to think that someone else is trying to get in your knickers."

"Oh, nice turn of phrase. You think that's what all men see in me?"

"No, of course not, I didn't mean that. You're clever, funny, beautiful, and could have any man you want. I'm sure as hell punching above my weight. But I have overwhelming urge to protect you from dick-heads like him." He stood up and walked over to me. "And I really did just want to surprise you. I missed spending time with you last weekend and wanted to make tonight really special. There was a plan, honestly, and a reason for turning up at work just so I could come here while you got ready."

"Why? You said you were coming to pick me up at seven?" it was my turn to be confused.

"I've booked us a meal Peckforton Castle. It's at least an hour away, so I needed to make sure we weren't late, to make our reservation for eight thirty." He paused, and I waited for him to go on. "And it was going to be a surprise, but I booked us a room. I was going to grab a change of clothes and put them in the car while you were in the shower. I've even bought your makeup and toothbrush from my place, so I just needed something for you to put on in the morning."

"Christ, Adam, you're a prize dick sometimes." He looked wounded. "Yes, it's a lovely idea, but do you have to be such a fucking control freak?" I sighed, not sure what else to say.

"I did warn you about that" he half smiled. "And you most definitely bring out the worst in me." He shuffled closer and took my hands in both of his. "These last few months have been amazing. I wanted to show you that I can be a romantic, and this isn't just about being your Dom. I thought I might try just being your boyfriend this weekend. See?" He pushed up his sleeve to show that he wasn't wearing the bracelet that I had given him at Christmas. It was a simple leather thong, with tiny silver beads spelling out the word 'Master' in morse code, and he had worn it tucked under his shirt sleeve every day since. It had taken a while to convince me that I could be what Adam wanted, and

I really didn't want to throw it all away because of a moment of pig-headedness – on both our parts.

"Will you at least come to dinner, and we'll talk about it?" he asked somewhat sheepishly "And if you're still pissed off at me, we don't have to stay."

"Well, we're not going to get there for half eight, are we? I'm not even dressed."

"I'll can call them – see if they'll hold the table" he smiled. "How quickly can you get ready?"

I looked at my watch and groaned in exasperation. "I'd better jump in a quick shower!"

29

We drove out past Nantwich, towards Tarporley, before picking up the tourist signs to Peckforton. We approached through huge wooden gates in a high stone wall, then followed the sweeping drive to the main entrance, and the car park beyond.

"Jesus, it really is a castle!" There was a dusting of snow on the grass in front of the building, which sparkled from the yellow lights set at ground level along the edge of the drive. Across the front of the building itself, there were uplighters hidden amount the plants, casting a golden light across the stone façade. The tall leaded windows shone with a warm and inviting glow.

Once inside, the entrance hall and reception area was a vast space, with red sandstone walls which were hung with huge tapestries, and an enormous iron chandelier hung on a heavy chain from the high ceiling. We were shown straight to our table in the restaurant, which was surprisingly modern by comparison. It was decorated in muted shades of pale duck egg blue and soft teal, which balanced the dark wooden furniture. Once seated the maître d' handed us each a menu and a wine list, while another waiter arrived to ask if we would like a drink from the bar.

"There aren't any prices" I leaned forward and whispered, having glanced through the menu. "The only ones marked are the additional supplements."

"Don't worry about it." Adam replied. "I booked a package - three course dinner, bed and breakfast. These places always have a quiet period in the New Year, so it wasn't too exorbitant. Just order what you want."

"What are you having?" I said without looking up. "I'm racking up extra charges already, and I've only looked at the starters and mains – blimey, the lamb sounds nice, but an extra seven quid's a bit much." I closed he menu and looked at Adam. "I'll have the ravioli and the chicken."

Just then the maître d' arrived back to take our orders. "The lady will have the savoury panna cotta with crab followed by the lamb with pea and goats cheese, and I'll have squid ink and chorizo risotto, then the pork with black pudding and apple, thank you." The man took the menus from Adam, nodding politely, although he hadn't written any of it down.

"And to drink, Sir?"

"I think we'll go with the Riesling, and a bottle of sparkling water too, thank you."

"Hmm, so much for not being the Dom tonight. You can't help it, can you?" I teased. "Thank you."

"Well, I know what you're like. I've told you, if you want something, just have it. You don't have to keep justifying every penny. If I couldn't afford to bring you, I wouldn't have booked it."

"I know, it just seems a lot. I dread to think how much the rooms cost, and I haven't even decided whether I've forgiven you. I might make you take me home yet."

"Well," he said just as the wine arrived, "You'd better decide pretty sharpish, because you're already half a bottle ahead of me, so I was planning on having at least half of this one." He tasted the wine, then gestured to the waiter, who poured us each a glass.

Adam's risotto arrived, black and glossy, with rocket and chorizo piled on top. I pulled a face – the dark colour of the rice didn't exactly make it look appetizing. "No, but it tastes bloody fantastic" he said, after swallowing his first forkful. "How's yours?"

"Absolutely divine. I do love crab."

"I know. I don't know why you didn't just order it in the first place?" Adam topped up my wine glass, then hovered with the bottle. "So, are we staying?"

"Well, it does seem a shame not to, given that you've paid for the night. Besides, I'm dying to see what the rooms are like."

"Thank fuck for that." He refilled his own glass, and leaned back in his chair. "I am sorry I embarrassed you – really."

"Yeah, well, maybe I did over-react, but I don't like being on the back foot like that. All you had to do was say you'd pick me up from work. There was no need to snog my face off in front of everyone. That was just cringe-worthy."

"It was a bit, wasn't it? I was waiting in my car, but then I recognized that knob Chris from the way you'd described him, and I don't know what came over me. Still, it could have been worse – I actually wanted to punch his lights out, but that wouldn't have helped either of us."

"No, it bloody wouldn't!" The waiter cleared our starters away, and my plate was soon replaced with the beautifully roasted rump of lamb, with a warm salad of peas and pea shoots, with mint and crumbly goats cheese. There was also a small side dish of roasted whole baby carrots and earthy beetroot with a honey glaze, and buttered new potatoes.

"Mm-mmm" I nodded enthusiastically, not wanting to speak with my mouth full. We ate in virtual silence, save the occasional appreciative noises as we enjoyed the gorgeous food. Afterwards, I leaned back in my chair with a sigh, and picked up my glass. "I can honestly say, that was the best lamb I've ever tasted. So much better than the chicken would have been. Thanks."

"Like I said, I don't know why you get so hung up on the price of things. It's only money. While I've got it to spare, just enjoy it, and if I can't afford it, I'll say so."

"So, are you loaded then, or what?" I asked, trying to make it sound like a joke, but I was nonetheless intrigued. The matter of finances had not yet come up in any conversation.

"God, no! I was left a bit of money when my Mum died about 8 years ago, so I put that down on the house, which means I'm fortunate enough to have a tiny mortgage. I know the house isn't very big, and some people wouldn't want to live that close to the town, but it suits me. It's big enough for one, and it's close enough to walk if I ever want to go out in town. It's a company car, so other than the bike, and a decent stereo, I've never spent a lot of money on 'stuff'. I like nice food, and going to gigs, but I save quite a bit. Why, would it make a difference?"

"Course not, I was just curious. You're really generous, and it's nice, but I do feel guilty sometimes. I mean I don't earn a bad wage for what

I do, but my mortgage payments take up a massive chunk every month, so after the bills have gone out, there isn't a lot left. I just have to be a bit careful, that's all. I can't afford to splash out on fancy dinners and hotels."

"Listen, if you're short of a few quid, you only have to ask. Like I said, I've got a bit tucked away for a rainy day, so just say if you need a hand."

"Honestly, I'm fine" I regretted saying anything. "I manage ok, until something goes wrong with the car, or the boiler, so some other bill comes in that I wasn't expecting. I've got a salary review in April, and fully intend to ask for a decent increase if things keep going the way they have been. That would certainly mean I could start putting away just a bit for a contingency fund, or even just for the holiday."

"Well, don't worry about the holiday" he said, "I didn't ask you with the idea that you'd have to pay for yourself. I'll cover the accommodation, and we don't have to spend a fortune eating out. As you know, I'm just as happy with fish and chips, or crackers and cheese and a bottle of red, as long as the company is decent. Now, are we going to order a pudding?" The waiter had arrived with dessert menus.

"I don't know – I'm not sure I can fit much more in. Erm, maybe the tropical one – the mango and passion fruit with the sorbet and coconut?" I handed my menu back to the waiter.

"And I'll have the tarte au citron, thanks. And two black coffees. If we can take those in the lounge, please?"

"Of course, Sir, please find a seat when you are ready, and I'll bring it to you there. Anything else? Would you prefer a liqueur coffee, or brandy maybe?"

"Why not. Hennessy VSOP if you've got it, or something similar. Babe?"

"Not for me" I shook my head. "I'm not much of a brandy drinker."

"Ok, how about something else then." He turned to the waiter "Disaronno please, with ice."

We enjoyed our desserts, then moved to the lounge where we settled on a deep knole sofa to one side of an inglenook fireplace, with a crackling log fire.

"I like the sofa" Adam said, nodding toward the solid wooden finials secured with ropes at the corners, and wiggling his eyebrows. "Medieval bondage furniture."

"Behave." I nudged him, as I spotted the waiter approaching with a tray. "Coffee's here."

30

The room was not disappointing. It was stunning, with period details including a high vaulted ceiling and tall leaded windows with stained glass panels. The décor was a mix of classic and contemporary, with soft furnishings in heavy velvet and brocade fabrics, and a deep pile carpet. There were prints of hunting scenes in heavy gilded frames and a bronze statue of a horse on the desk by the window. The bed was the biggest I had ever seen, and so high that there was a small step at each side, to facilitate climbing onto the luxurious fine white linens and a mountain of deep feather pillows.

"Wow, it's beautiful!" I flopped onto the bed, laying on my back and admiring the ceiling which was painted a dark midnight blue, and scattered with gold stars which glinted in the lamplight.

"Does that mean I'm forgiven?" Adam sat on the edge of the be beside me. He reached down to slip off my stilettos and rubbed my feet and massaged my toes. "I don't know how you wear those things – they must cripple you."

"Hmm, but if it means I get a sympathy foot-rub from time to time, it's worth it" I closed my eyes, relaxing as he worked his hands over my foot and ankle, then began to massage my calf.

"Well, if you get undressed, I could give you a proper massage if you like." He picked up the other leg and began kneading the other calf muscle. "Do you fancy that?"

"That sounds good." I opened my eyes and sat up. Adam got off the bed and held out his hand to me. I stepped down into his arms and we shared a slow, melting kiss, his arms around me, holding me tight against his body.

"Take your clothes off. I'll see if there's some body lotion in the bathroom." He left the room, and I undressed, hanging my dress in the wardrobe.

"This should do" he returned from the bathroom holding a towel and two miniature bottles. "Almond shower oil"

I went to use the loo, and when I came back, Adam had spread a large towel on the bed and turned off the lights, leaving on a small brass desk lamp, which cast a warm golden glow across the room. I lay face down on the towel which he had laid out on top of the bed, while he undressed, hanging his suit in the wardrobe, then climbing onto the bed beside me. He opened the bottle of oil and poured some onto his hands, before smoothing it over my back and shoulders.

He started and the back of my neck, massaging the sides of my neck and working his way across my shoulders and down to my mid back. He squirted more of the almond scented oil on to my back and worked downwards in circular movements. He used his fingers, palms and fists to add a variety of sensations, with long slow stokes, with just enough pressured down either side of my spine. He worked slowly down my back, kneading my buttocks and sliding oiled fingers along my cleft before pressing one finger inside my back passage. Then his hands moved downwards, paying attention to the junction where my thigs met just below my bum, again just pressing lightly against either side of my pussy, then down my legs, rolling the muscles of my thighs and calves between his hands. When he reached my feet, again applying more of the oil, he lifted each foot in turn, working over the ankle, pressing his fingers in circles along arch and ball of the foot, and between my toes.

"Turn over babe" he whispered, lowing my foot back down on the bed.

Now he worked back up the front of my legs, stroking my inner thighs, his fingertips barely touching my outer lips and eliciting a moan or pleasure. Then he moved up and over my hips and belly to my chest, before working down each arm in turn. He lifted each hand, spreading the oil over my wrists and palms, before sliding over each finger in turn. Adam poured some more of the oil on to his hands, and placed them on my collar bones, working of the muscles either side of my neck then sliding his hands down to my breasts, kneading softly, pressing my breasts together, his thumbs gliding over my nipples. It felt so erotic, and I was breathing harder when he shifted position and lifted each leg in turn, bending my knees and letting my thighs fall open.

Now his hands moved over my hips and down my outer thighs, before returning upwards on the inside, his thumbs working upwards towards my pussy, and pressing inwards, as if pushing my swollen lips together. The pressure against all the nerve endings around my labia made me moan again, although he had still not directly touched my clit. I opened my thighs wider, lifting my hips and offering myself to him. He parted my folds and slipped two fingers inside me. I was soaking wet, and whimpered, raising my hips higher to take his fingers deeper. Instead he withdrew them, and positioned himself between my legs, his erection nudging against my opening.

We kissed, his tongue lightly brushing against my lips at first before slipping into my mouth to dance with mine. My arms wrapped around his back as he entered me. He set a pace that was slow and languid, rotating his hips against mine, his pubic bone creating just enough pressure against by clit that I was soon climbing towards an orgasm.

"God, that feels so good" I moaned breathlessly, and just a few moments later my body was wracked with a powerful orgasm. I dug my fingers into his buttocks, as if trying to pull him deeper inside me, but Adam carried on his slow rhythmic grinding, until my clit became too sensitive, and I had to beg him to stop.

He rolled off me, and I lay panting, while my pussy throbbed. He kissed me softly, stroking my face, and nuzzling against my cheek, and I realized that was probably the first time we had made love in the true sense of the words. I felt suddenly overwhelmed with emotion and turned away from him onto my side, fearing that I was about to give way to tears.

Adam kissed the back of my neck, his arm reaching around to cup my breast, and I could feel he still had a raging hard-on, which nudged against my backside. I pressed back against him and felt his erection sliding up and down between my buttocks. Then I raised one leg slightly, shifting my weight slightly over on to my front, and allowing him to enter me from behind. The penetration wasn't deep from that angle, but each thrust pushed against the front wall of my pussy, rubbing against by G-spot. He was moving faster now, and I rolled fully onto my front. As he lifted himself off the bed to adjust his position, I pushed myself up onto my hands and knees.

"Fuck, you're so sexy" he moaned, as he buried his cock inside me from behind. He had one hand on my hip, the other was on my shoulder, holding me in position as he moved. He thrust hard, then withdrew almost completely, before burying himself up to the hilt again. After a few moments, his thrusting slowed, and he ran his hand down my back and gripped my buttocks with both hands, spreading them apart. Then he ran his fingers up and down my cleft, coating them with a mixture of the almond oil and my own juices, and pushed a finger inside my tightest opening. He moved his finger in and out, before slowly inserting a second digit, and pressing downwards. With two fingers inside my back passage, he began slowly thrusting his cock in my pussy. I felt so full, and the pressure inside was incredible. I was going to cum again really soon.

"Oh Adam, I'm so close" I panted "please don't stop." He scissored his fingers inside me, stretching and pushing in and out as if fucking me there, while his cock remained still inside me, his hips pressed tight against my backside.

"Feels good, doesn't it?" he said softly, and I moaned my agreement. "You have no idea how much I want to cum here."

"Yes," I whispered. "I want you to."

Adam stopped, not sure whether he had heard or perhaps misunderstood. "Tell me babe, what do you want."

"I want you to put your cock in me. There." I craned my neck around to meet his gaze. "Please, I'd like to try. Just don't hurt me."

Adam stepped off he bed, and went to his bag, where he retrieved a bottle of lube. "Are you sure baby? I need you to be certain."

"Yes, I… just get on with it before I change my mind. Be gentle." I closed my eyes and felt the cold lube drip down my cleft, and Adams fingers working it inside me, opening me up to accept his cock. He took the bottle again, this time sliding it over his shaft.

"Relax, I'll go slowly" he positioned himself at my back entrance, pushing the tip of his cock until he felt the resistance of the tight ring of muscle. "Just breath, and focus on letting me in baby. Relax your muscles and push against me."

My body resisted the invasion, making it feel like there was no way I could ever take him, but I wasn't going to give up that easily. I took another deep breath and blew it out, focusing on accepting his cock. Soon he was all the way inside me, and it felt like I was going to be ripped apart. Adam hissed out a breath as he pulled back, then eased inside again. I felt totally invaded and sweat began broke out on my neck and forehead. He began rocking into me slowly, and I focused on the sensation of fulness, as my body grew accustomed to his length. He was still being cautious not to thrust too hard or too fast, but kept up a steady rhythm, as I relaxed and began to enjoy the feeling of fullness, and push against him.

"Shit babe, I'm going to cum. Do you want me to stop?" Adam was breathless now.

"No, please, I want you to cum inside me."

He didn't need telling twice, and a wretched cry tore out of him, as I pushed back to meet his thrusts. As if from somewhere in the distance, I heard my own moans, and felt his heat explode inside me, followed by the softening of his grip against my waist.

Then came the tears.

I fell forward onto the bed and sobbed into the duvet. Adam pulled me to him, his arm wrapping around my waist, while one hand stroked my hair.

"It's ok sweetheart, you're ok. Did I hurt you?" He lifted my hand and kissed my palm.

I shook my head, sniffing, and trying to stifle the sobs, as hot tears rolled down my cheeks. "Shh, it's ok. Let it out."

Eventually the tears stopped, and Adam spoke first, cradling me in his arms.

"I'm sorry, I didn't mean to hurt you. I should never have done that. You've had too much to drink, and I shouldn't have pushed you."

"You didn't hurt me – not really. I just feel a bit wrung out and emotional. I'd been worrying about that and building it up in my head. I didn't expect to feel so overwhelmed."

"Come on, a bath should help." He was off the bed, and went into the en-suite bathroom, and then I heard the bath running, followed the sound of the loo flushing. He came back to the bedroom, and taking me by the hand, pulled me off the bed and into his arms. "Do you want me to leave you to it? I could make you a hot chocolate, or call room service, if you want something stronger?"

"Will you get in with me?" I looked up into those blue eyes, which at that moment were full of love. I got into the tub, and he climbed in behind me, cradling me against his chest, as I let the hot water soothe any soreness away.

31

When I awoke the next morning, the unmistakable pale blue-white light coming from the crack in the curtains told me that there had been snow in the night. Adam lay breathing heavily beside me, so I climbed down from the bed, and went to pull back the heavy curtains. The view was breathtakingly beautiful. Our room was on the second floor at the back of the hotel, and the manicured grounds sloped down to a high stone wall, with nothing but fields beyond, to the edge of a forest. Everything was covered in fresh pristine snow, which softened the edges of borders and paths, as if the whole scene were a cake, draped in fondant icing.

I dropped tea-bags into two cups, and switched the kettle on, before going to use the bathroom.

"Ow, fuck!" for a moment I'd forgotten the night before, but when I sat on the loo, I got a sudden reminder.

"Zoe?" Adam tapped on the door, "You ok?"

"Shit. Sorry, yes. I'll be out in a min. Finish the tea."

I emerged a few minutes later to find Adam sat in one of the deep velvet button-backed chairs, looking out at the snow. He turned, genuine concern on his face. "Are you sure you're ok?"

"Yeah, just a bit sore" I blushed "And a bit of an upset tummy I think – I don't know if that's a thing after anal, or if it was just the rich food last night." I lowered myself somewhat gingerly into the other chair and picked up my cup of tea.

"I hope it's not too uncomfortable. I've got some paracetamol, if you think that might help, but we don't have to rush to do anything. Do you want me to order breakfast in the room instead of going down to the restaurant?" he asked.

"No, honestly, I'll be fine. It's not that bad, I just wasn't sure what to expect. What time's breakfast – I'm bloody starving."

32

After a huge cooked breakfast, we moved to the lounge once more, where we enjoyed another pot of coffee in front of the roaring fire.

"Well, I was hoping we could have a walk around the estate this morning" Adam said, "But I hadn't planned for snow. Is there anything you want to do instead? Anywhere you fancy going?"

"Not really. We could just head back if you like."

"Or I've got an idea. We could head over to Northwich, there's a big motorbike clothing and accessories place. It's only about twenty minutes from here. Get you a lid and a jacket for starters? They tend to have a few bargains this time of year, before the new ranges come out ready for summer."

"OK, but only if we can find something pretty cheap. I don't imagine it's something I'm going to want to do very often. I'm quite nervous about the idea of getting on the back of one of those things, if I'm honest."

"You'll love it – trust me" he grinned.

The main roads were pretty much clear of snow, and just under half an hour later, we arrived at J & S

Accessories. It was huge, and I had no idea there was such a choice of motorcycle clothing, or how much the prices varied. Two hours later, I was fully kitted out. We got a lightweight waterproof jacket with armour in the shoulders and elbows, in black with panels of baby blue, a pair of black short boots, black Kevlar jeans and of course full-face helmet. Adam pulled a face when I chose one with silver and baby blue floral decals on the black background. Apparently, it had taken him several months to track down the R1200GS Triple Black, along with the matching black aluminium luggage, so he wasn't keen on my colourful girly accessories. As I pointed out, if I was going to ride pillion, I was going to do it in style, thank you very much, whether it ruined his image or not.

Everything we picked was in the sale at less than half the original price, and Adam persuaded the assistant to throw in a pair of gloves for free, especially after he also ordered an intercom set so we could communicate while riding. He paid for the lot, after agreeing that I could give him the money for the helmet if I really wanted to, and we set off home.

33

We'd only just arrived back at Adam's house, when my phone rang. It was Angie, and she sounded stressed.

"Hey hun, you know you said I could come and stay if I wanted? Well, I'm on the way – I'm at Stafford Services. I don't know how far that is from you, but are you at home?"

"I wasn't, but I soon will be. Is everything ok?" I asked

"Not really. I'll fill you in when I get there. Thanks, lovely. See you in a bit."

"Shit." I turned to Adam, who was making a cuppa. "I'm sorry, I've got to go. That was Ange, and she's on her way to my place. I don't know the details, but something must have happened to make her want to leave suddenly. Can you run me home?"

"Course. I hope she's ok. Do you need me to do anything?"

"I don't think so – I need to find out what's happened."

We arrived at my front door less that half and hour later. "Thanks Adam, I'll call you later" I gave him a quick kiss as he handed me my bag, then waved him off as I opened my front door.

Angie arrived about 20 minutes later, her eyes red-rimmed and puffy. I gave her a hug as she stepped into the hallway, but she pushed me away.

"Don't, you'll only set me off again!" she smiled as she brushed away the tears that threatened. "I'm sorry, have I ruined your Saturday night plans?"

"Never mind that, come in and I'll make us a brew." I took her bag and dropped it at the bottom of the stairs, then flicked the kettle on. When I followed her into the lounge with two mugs of tea, Ange had taken off her boots, and was curled up on the sofa, a cushion hugged to her chest.

"So, what's happened? Are you ok? Or is that a daft question?"

"He's a lying, cheating scumbag, that's all. He's been shagging Verity, one of the branch staff from Gloucester. He swore blind there was no-one else. We both agreed we'd keep it amicable and not start dating anyone else until the finances were settled so I could move out. Instead, he's found some younger model, with 'a decent rack', apparently. It was so obvious when he started buying new clothes, trying to look trendy, and growing his hair."

"You're kidding" I laughed "Mark's growing his hair? I'm sorry, I shouldn't laugh, but he always hated long hair on blokes."

"Oh, it gets worse," she dunked a biscuit in her tea. "He's got a top-knot … a bloody man-bun! He thinks he looks like one of those premier league footballers, except he's too fat and bow-legged to look sporty, and his the nearest he's got to designer clothes is Top Man."

Soon we were both laughing at how ludicrous it all seemed, although Ange was obviously hurt and felt betrayed.

"I suppose I didn't think he had it in him" she said, after a while. "He was always a bit of a nerd, and he wasn't very confident with women when we met. I suppose I hadn't really noticed how much we've both changed."

"I'm so sorry, I wish I knew what else to say. You know you're better off without him."

"I know. It just feels so shitty. You know I said he was really boring in bed? Well apparently, she's more exciting than me - more adventurous in the bedroom. Bitch!" she spat.

"Oh Jesus, that really sucks."

"Ha! I dare say she does *that* better than me too!"

Later I took Ange up to my spare room, and after taking down the ironing board, and removing my tights and knickers from the rack on the radiator, I got fresh linen from the airing cupboard to make up the bed.

"I'm so grateful hun, it's just for a few days, until I decide what to do." She sniffed.

"Nonsense, what are friends for. But I don't suppose there's much you can do. Even if he wasn't seeing this girl, you already knew it was over between you. Here." I sat down on the bed and passed her a box of tissues. "Maybe he's just having a mid-life crisis, and it makes him feel young again, or who knows, maybe she'll give him the babies he wants. Whatever happens, it isn't your problem anymore, and it's given you the shove you needed to get out."

"I suppose." she blew her nose loudly. "I just need him to get the house valued now. I can't afford to walk away without a penny and start all over again."

"Too right. That needs sorting asap. Can you sort out the valuation from here? I mean you'll probably need a solicitor, but hopefully you can come to some arrangement between you, if he's still being reasonable."

"Oh, I've told him he needs to get a couple of agents in this week, and I want to know who they are, and copies of the valuations in writing. It needs sorting, before his bimbo moves in and stakes her claim. As far as I'm concerned, I don't care if she gets pregnant, then dumps him and tries to take the lot."

My mobile was ringing, and it was Adam, just making sure Angie was ok. I left her to unpack her bag, and took the call downstairs.

"Oh, you know - hurt, angry, bitter," I said "Just what you'd expect after being with someone for over a decade then finding out they were shagging someone younger and with bigger tits. I think she'll be ok, though it doesn't feel like it right now."

"I'm sure. Sounds like an arsehole." Adam had a very strict moral code, and one thing you didn't do in his book was cheat. No matter what the circumstances.

"Do you want to come over tonight, or maybe we could all go out for lunch tomorrow, so Ange can meet you?"

"Hmm, not sure that's a good idea. I think you should probably concentrate on your friend, and give her a bit of TLC, and I'll give you a call tomorrow night. Maybe if things have settled down, I could come over one night in the week and say hello. For now though, if she's anti-men, I don't want to inadvertently end up in the firing line, even if it isn't aimed at me personally."

"Ok sweetheart. I'm sorry."

"No need to apologise. Speak to you soon, sexy. Love you."

34

On Wednesday Adam came over with a takeaway curry and a bottle of white wine, along with some beers. He and Angela seemed to get on really well. He was charming and attentive, while she was in a much better mood, and positively flirty.

"So, have you told her about the job?" he asked me, while I gathered up the cartons for the bin.

"What job?" Ange asked, sloshing the last of the wine into her glass.

"He means the job at my place. The Supervisor or Team Leader, or call it what you will. I mentioned it the other week, but it wouldn't be any good for you. You can do so much better. That's even if you decided to stay here for a bit."

"Oh right. No, I haven't decided where I'm going to go yet. It depends how quickly Mark can come up with a figure, and where I can afford to rent. I suppose it would be loads cheaper up here, would it? What are rental prices like compared to Exeter?"

"Probably about half what you'd pay down there" replied Adam. "Besides, it will depend on where you find work, I presume. What do you do first, find a job then rent somewhere to live nearby, or get a house then find work in the area?"

"You could stay here and register with a couple of agencies locally?" I suggested. "You don't need to worry about rent or anything, if you can just chip in towards food and bills. Have you got loads of friends in Exeter or stuff you don't want to leave behind?"

"No, not really. We went out with work colleagues, and most of them were other couples. There's nothing I need to go back there for if I'm honest."

"Well," Adam chipped in "It seems obvious to me - if the job is something you could do, even if it pays less than you're used to, at least you would have something to live off for now, and a roof over your head until you find something better. I mean if you've got the house and financial settlement to sort out, the last thing you want to do is add more stress trying to find a job and a place to stay at the same time."

"And you'd really be helping me out, if you'd at least come for an interview and have a look round?" I added "I don't know how much more I could get in the way of salary, because you're so over-qualified, but maybe I could tweak the job spec and sell it to the MD that you could do so much more. We've been saying for two years that we want to implement new telephone handling software, and you could manage all that techy stuff, and training."

My brain was working overtime now, and I was thinking out loud. "That's it, if I pitch it as maybe a twelve-month contract, sort of like a consultancy role? You could get the new systems in place, recruit some call-centre staff just on orders and payments, and train everyone up to a new set of targets. That way I can work on the Customer Service side and get a dedicated person in place for the escalated queries, and I can still do the data management, the debt analysis, and the fraud investigation stuff. What do you reckon?"

"I dunno. I'm not sure I want to work in a call centre again. Been there, done that, you know?" She shrugged "I suppose it wouldn't hurt to have a look at what you're doing at the moment, and I could at least stay here, and it would mean I could pay my way."

"And what's a year? It'll fly by. You can get to know the area, see if it's somewhere you could settle. I'll talk to Mike, the MD tomorrow, see if I can sound him about a salary deal. Ooh, I'm so excited!"

"Hold your horses!" exclaimed Ange "I haven't agreed to anything yet. You speak to your boss and let me know what he says, then I'll give it some thought. No promises though, ok?"

"Listen ladies, I'd better go" Adam stood up and went to grab his coat. "I've got work in the morning, and so have you, wench. Don't stay up all night hatching plans and getting your hopes up. This boss of yours may not even go for the idea."

"I know, I know." I followed him towards the front door. "Thanks for coming over."

"No worries. Are you coming at the weekend?"

"Yep, I'll text you nearer."

"Good. Now come here." He pulled me to him, and we kissed for several minutes. "I've been wanting to do that since I got here."

35

The next day I sent an email to Chris, formally inviting him for an interview. I couldn't not really, although I was praying I could persuade Mike to pay a bit more for the right person. He didn't rate Chris any more than I did, so if it came to a choice, I was sure I could swing things in Angie's favour. I set up the interview for Monday and needless to say, Chris accepted the appointment within seconds.

On Friday I looked through the dozen applications I'd had for telephone call handlers, and sorted in to Yes/No/Maybe piles. I planned to take them home with me, and maybe get Ange's take on things, but wasn't sure that was strictly ethical, given that she hadn't got the job yet. I stopped at the supermarket and grabbed a bottle of wine and some milk, and headed home.

"Hey hun, I'm in the kitchen." Ange called to me as I walked in the door. "I made dinner. Or have you got plans?"

"No, that's great. I didn't want to leave you on your own, so I told Adam I'll go over tomorrow some time."

"Don't go messing up your routine for my benefit. Seriously Zoe, I don't want to get in the way of your love life, and I certainly don't need babysitting. If you want me out of the way, I can always go to the pictures or something."

"You're fine" I laughed "I don't expect you to make yourself scarce. Like I said, we usually spend the weekend at his, and sometimes he comes here mid-week if it's not too late but doesn't usually stay over then. I have a couple of things to do in the morning, then I'll stay there until Sunday. I should be back around teatime, but don't worry about cooking or anything – you just fend for yourself. I'll let you know if I'm going to be late, but otherwise I'll see you when I see you."

"No worries. I might go and check out the shops. I didn't bring much with me, so could do with some basics."

"Well, I would say help yourself if you want to borrow anything to wear, but that's not going to work – what are you, a size 10?"

"More like an 8 at the minute – I haven't been eating much just lately. But I feel loads better this week. I've decided to move on. Fuck him. Just as soon as I get some cash. We did loads of work on the house after I moved in, so it's worth way more than it was. I just want a percentage of however much it's increased in value. I'm not greedy, but we both put our money in to the cost of the kitchen extension, and the re-wiring and new bathrooms, and having the drive block paved, stuff like that. Why should he reap the rewards, while I walk away with nothing to show for all those years?"

"Hmm, you're right. You'd better chase up those valuations, before his new bimbo gets her claws in, and persuades him otherwise." We ate dinner, then had a choc-ice from the freezer. "By the way, your interview is at 3.30 on Monday. Is that ok?"

"Course. How many others are you interviewing?" she asked.

I told her about Chris, but decided not to mention what a creep he was, or about him asking me out, and the inappropriate comments. If she did take the job, Ange would have to work with him, and it would be unfair of me to colour her opinion of him.

36

On Saturday I was up early, and did some laundry, which Ange said she'd put in the dryer for me later. I decided to call in on Kate at the shop and tell her about our night away. I was weirdly nervous but excited to tell her what had happened that night. I'd been thinking about it a lot.

"Morning lovely, I bought hot chocolate!" she greeted me with her usual warm smile as I closed the door behind me, then came over to give me a hug."

"Thanks Zoe," she said taking both steaming cups from me. "There's someone I'd like you to meet." She took my hand and led me to the back of the shop, through the door into the tiny workroom which doubled as an office. "Sir, I'd like you to meet my friend Zoe. Zoe, this is Lee."

As he stood up from the desk, I suddenly realized I was meeting her Dom, and tried to remember how she had greeted Adam when they met. Instead, I stared up at him, panicked for a moment, then kind of curtsied. For a moment he seemed somewhat confused, but then smiled and held out his hand.

"Zoe, it's pleasure to meet you. Kate has mentioned you often." He was drop-dead gorgeous, with Mediterranean good looks and the darkest eyes I'd ever seen, which seemed to be studying me intently.

"You too" I managed I managed to mutter, blushing furiously, before Kate took my arm and steered me back towards the shop.

"Oh god, I'm so sorry – he must think I'm a complete idiot!" I said as soon as we were out of earshot.

"Don't be silly, it's fine - I did kind of ambush you. And I suppose he is a bit intimidating until you get to know him."

"I can't believe I actually curtsied!" I laughed, covering my crimson face in shame. "Listen, I only popped in for a chat, but I can come back another time, when you're on your own."

"There's no need, honestly. I'm crap with paperwork, so Sir comes in to do the accounts for me once a month. He says it's because I have a creative brain, not a practical one, but I think that's being kind. He'll have his head down for an hour or so."

"Ok, if you're sure. I wanted to tell you about last weekend. Adam took me away to a hotel. We had a meal and stayed overnight. It was fantastic." I told her about the castle, and the amazing food, and the massage. "And so anyway, I did it. *We had anal sex.*" I whispered it, although there was no-one else in the shop.

"Wow, good for you. And how was it? Not that I want the gory details or anything, but was it ok?" she asked. "Not too painful?"

"No, surprisingly not. I'd had a couple drinks, and the massage must've helped. I was feeling so relaxed and horny … I actually asked him to. He was fucking me from behind, and it just seemed like a natural progression. I just wanted to try, for him really." Kate nodded her understanding. "It was uncomfortable at first, but we shared a bath afterwards, and that soothed any pain." I took a sip of my drink. "I'll tell you what though, having a poo in the morning was a bit an eye-opener. It didn't half sting, and stuff came out of me that I'm not sure I could describe!" Kate cracked up, nearly choking on her hot chocolate. I was so at ease with her, it felt good to be able to be that candid.

"Jeez, thanks for sharing!" she snorted with laughter "Yeah, it can be a bit messy. You've got two choices, either get him to use a condom, or tell him he can visit, but can't finish there." She shrugged, laughing, just as her Dom came through from the back room.

"Sounds like you too are having fun. What's the joke?" We looked at each other, trying to keep our faces straight, and I blushed again.

"Oh, nothing important Sir – just girly stuff." she said, winking at me.

"I should go." I stood up to leave. "I'm sorry if I disturbed you."

"Nonsense. I'm glad you popped by." He put his hand into his back pocket, then taking out his wallet, extracted a business card which he held out to me. "You should join us for dinner one night. Kate is an excellent cook. Perhaps you'd ask your Dom to give me a call."

"That would be lovely." I remembered to bow my head this time, lowering my eyes as Kate had done. "I will, thank you, Sir."

"Good." He was much taller than Kate, and he placed a hand on her head, looking down as he stroked her hair. She closed her eyes and smiled, her body melting against him, as I left the shop.

I drove straight to Adam's, excited to tell him that we had been invited for dinner by Kate's Dom. I really wanted to see how the relationship dynamic worked for them. He had seemed quite formal, and yes, intimidating. I'd also picked up the fact that she really did call him Sir, both to his face, and when talking about him. Adam was just … Adam. Unless we were actually "playing" as he liked to call it. I couldn't imagine being that way all the time.

Adam was in the living room when I arrived. There were several freshly ironed shirts on the back of the door, and he was sat on the sofa pairing socks from the laundry.

"Hey sweetpea, you ok? How's Angie doing?"

"She's fine. I think she's going into town today for a few bits, and she's lined up a box set to watch. I called in to see Kate on the way over, to tell her about last weekend. You don't mind, do you?"

"Mind? Why, what have you been saying about me?" then it must have dawned on him what I meant. "Oh, I take it you didn't just talk about the food then. It's fine babe."

"Good. And I met her Dom, his names Lee. I got all flustered and didn't know what to say to him, but he seems nice. Actually, he's invited us for dinner." I took the business card out of my back pocket and handed it to Adam. "He says you should call him and arrange it sometime."

"Lee Cirillo, MBBS, MRCOG" he read the card "Presume he's doctor of some sort?"

"No idea - Kate never mentioned what he does. He was in the back office looking at the books and sorting some paperwork. He's not what I imagined though – he's at least ten years older than her. Not that it matters. The way she looked at him, honestly, she worships him."

"Hmm? Oh well, I'll give him a call, although I might Google him first. Now, come here wench."

I went and wrapped my arms around Adam's neck, and we kissed for several minutes. "Wait, where's your collar?" he asked, looking down at my bare neck.

"Shit, I'm sorry." Adam looked seriously angry, and he walked into the kitchen, his fists clenched at his sides. "I just forgot, what with having Ange to stay, and being excited to go and talk to Kate. It won't happen again."

"No. It won't." he glared at me. "Kneel down."

I did as I was told, placing my hands on his thighs and licking my lips, expecting him to drop his jogging trousers so he could use my mouth. Instead, he walked through the kitchen, then I heard him unlock the door to the garage. A few moments later he came back into the room, with what looked like a leather strap or belt wrapped around his fist.

"Stand up." he said, coldly. "This won't be as comfortable as yours, but maybe that will teach you not to forget again." He stood behind me, then wrapped the strap around my neck, securing the buckle at the back. It was made of stiff black leather, and although it wasn't too tight, it was wide enough that it prevented me from lowering my chin, and similarly, if I tried to raise my head upwards, the buckle dug into my neck at the back. "Now, take your jeans off."

I struggled to get my boots off because I couldn't look down, but eventually I stood, wearing just a t-shirt and my underwear. He took my hand and led me through to the garage, when he lifted the punch bag off the hook. Next, he pulled the t-shirt up over my head, then slowly removed my bra and knickers, so that I was naked except for the collar. He took a pair of leather cuffs from the cupboard, fastened them around my wrists, and lifted my arms to fasten me to the chain above my head.

"Please, I just forgot. Sir, I'm sorry." He spanked me. "Ow!" I shrieked, more in shock than in pain at first, but he did it again, harder, on the other cheek. "No, please."

He stood in front of me, looking at me with such disappointment, that I wanted to cry.

"You disobeyed me." he said, "Do you understand that?"

"I know - I just forgot" the first tears leaked down my cheek.

"You forgot. Because you arrived here thinking about yourself, instead of thinking about me, and how you should behave." He took out the flogger.

"Shit. Please, don't hurt me. Sir?"

He looked even more disappointed. "Why would you think I'd hurt you? I don't want to cause you physical pain sweetpea. I don't get off on that. Besides, you liked this last time I used this." As he said it, he raised his arm and brought the flogger down across my backside, once, twice. I gritted my teeth and let out a hiss, as the blows heated my skin.

"There, that's not so bad, is it?" I shook my head, as he began to swish the flogger back and forth, criss-crossing the blows against my bum and thighs, until I moaned. He caressed my heated backside, and I held my breath as he squeezed the hot flesh. His hand slid between my legs and a I groaned as he pressed against my opening and slid two fingers inside me.

"So, tell me, is it the sting from the flogger that turns you on? Or just the mix of anticipation tinged with a little fear?" I closed my eyes and bit my lip, and he brought his hand down hard against my bum "Tell me!"

"I don't know. Both." I squeezed my eyes shut as more tears threatened.

He stood in front of me now and kissed me as his hands worked over my breasts, pinching my nipples, then moving over my hips and pulling me against him, his hands digging into my fiery buttocks. I moaned, trying to press myself closer, but as he moved away, the chain holding my hands above my head stopped me from following him. He stepped backwards, watching as my eyes searched his for what was coming next. He went back to the cupboard at the back of the garage and took out a toy. It was purple and fitted into his palm, and as he turned it on, he held it out for me to see. It had two fingers like the ears on my favourite rabbit vibrator, but there was no shaft. He held it towards my pussy, barely touching, so I could feel just the slightest tickle – almost like a movement of air against my clit. I tipped my hips forward to press against the vibrating fingers, but he pulled away.

"Uh oh, not so fast." He chuckled, then went back to the cupboard. When he came back behind me, he unfastened and removed the thick black leather collar.

"Thanks" I sighed "That was so uncomfortable, I couldn't move my neck."

He rubbed at the back of my neck where the buckle had been, while kissing my shoulder and the side of my neck. I craned my neck around to meet his mouth and his tongue flicked over my lips.

"Open" he said softly, pressing something which I hadn't seen against my mouth. "Wider." It felt like a rubber circle or tube, and he pushed it into my mouth, then quickly more straps wrapped around the back of my head, pulling me backwards.

I tried to say "what the fuck?" as he fastened the buckle at the back of my head, but it just came out as incoherent muffled noises. The gag held my mouth open wide, and as I explored it with my tongue, I found it difficult to swallow my own spit.

"What was that?" he stood facing me now, and slid two fingers through the gag, pressing against the back of my tongue, until I gagged, and pulled my head away.

"Aargh, yeg, YEG!" I yanked my wrists against their restraints, suddenly panicked that I couldn't even say my safeword with that horrible rubber restriction in my mouth, but he wrapped his arms around me, cradling my head until I relaxed.

"Sshh, I know." He kissed my neck and cheeks, and I tried to press my face to his, unable to kiss him back. "Here, use this instead of your colours." He put something into my hand, and I looked up to see a D-shaped plastic toy covered with bells, like the sleighbells we used to have in primary school music lessons. I shook it, as much as I could with the restricted movement in my wrists.

"Good. Now listen to me carefully." As he said it, he turned on he vibrator again and held it in front of my crotch. "You don't get to cum until I say so. Understand?" I nodded, and he pressed the toy against my aching pussy. I let out a moan, closing my eyes. The fingers buzzed and pulsed against me, and it wasn't long before I was wriggling and rocking my hips against it, my breath coming in short pants. He could tell I was getting close, and glared at me, his head on one side, with the "don't you dare" look I now recognised. I shook the sleighbells, and he immediately withdrew his hand with the vibrator.

"That's my good girl." he said, his hand cupping my face. I leaned my cheek against his hand and closed my eyes, longing to feel his mouth on mine, but instead he stepped back, and pushed his fingers between my legs and into my pussy. I tried to open my legs, but that meant going up on to my tip toes, and I couldn't hold the position. Then Adam raised his fingers to his face, inhaling deeply the scent of my musk, before pushing his fingers into my mouth. They were wet with the tang of my own juices as he pressed them against my tongue, then when he withdrew his fingers, a string of saliva followed and hung from my mouth, falling down my chin, and dripping onto my chest.

"You look so hot and desperate, drooling down yourself. I'm so fucking hard right now!" As he spoke, he put his hand inside his sweatpants and winced as he adjusted his erection. "Now, where were we?"

He pressed the vibrator against me again, at the same time with his other hand he plucked at my nipples, rolling them between his fingers and thumb until they ached. The slow build was excruciating, and again, he kissed and nibbled at my neck, and I longed to be able to meet his mouth and kiss him properly. Again, I was climbing, trying to switch my attention away from the buzz against my clit. I moaned, feeling totally helpless to do anything but give in to the pleasure, until once again I was shaking those bloody sleighbells for all I was worth. Fuck it, I wasn't going to let him win to his stupid game.

This time he left me just hanging there, and went into the house, returning with a glass of water. He drank about half of it, watching me intently. I closed my eyes. My hands were tingling from the cuffs, and my shoulders ached form being in the unnatural position. I realized that I had been slumped, letting the chain take my body weight, so I stood up a little taller, relieving the weight from my shoulders, and tilted my head up, with a look of pure defiance now.

"God you're even more beautiful when you're angry" he said, smiling. "But I've told you, you won't win." He turned the vibrator on once more, and within just a few moments I was whimpering, rocking my hips back and forth against. This time he kept pulling it away, then he'd press again, then press it to change the rhythm, which went from a constant buzz through a cycle of pulsing, then it would stop, and build slowly from slow to intense, then stop and start slowly again. As much as I tried to switch off and think of anything but my impending orgasm, the constant change of pace kept my attention firmly focused on my pussy.

Adam grinned as I started to shake the sleighbells, but he didn't take the toy away. This time he turned it down to low, and settled it against my clit, holding it firmly in place. I shook my head, groaning against the awful rubber gag, lifting up on my toes to try and escape from the vibration, which was almost too much to bear. I cried out around the gag, saliva flowing freely and running down my chin. I half dropped, half threw the sleighbells on the floor and pulled on the wrist cuffs as every muscle in my body tensed. I tried to close my legs, squeezing my eyes shut tightly, then crying out around the rubber gag, biting down until my jaw ached.

When Adam took the vibrator away, I slumped with my head down on my chest, strands of drool dripping on to the rubber mat on the floor and my own wetness coating my thighs. He reached up and unhooked the carabiner which fastened the cuffs to the chain in the ceiling, and I dropped to my knees on the mat, my shoulders screaming with pain. I looked up to see Adam's hand wrapped around his cock, his fist moving frantically up and down over his length. He was breathing hard, and the veins in his neck stood out. I lifted myself up off my heels and tried to unfasten the cuffs, but at that moment, he looked down at me and groaned through gritted teeth as he emptied his balls. Thick jets of cum sprayed onto my face and chest, then hit the floor, the rest coating his fist as he rolled his foreskin over his swollen glans and squeezed out the last drops. He leaned back against the wall, his eyes closed for a moment, as he recovered his composure, then tucked himself back into his sweatpants, and looked down at me, still kneeling on the floor, gagged and cuffed.

38

Adam knelt down beside me, first undoing the buckle that held the gag in my mouth, then the leather cuffs on my wrists. He sat on the floor, pulling me onto his lap, where he I sat for several moments, while he massaged my shoulders and neck then my hands and wrists.

"That was horrible." I spoke first, struggling to get up off the floor, but he held me tightly to him.

"Tell me." He spoke softly, then after a moment repeated himself. "Tell me what it was that you hated, sweetpea." He lifted my chin to meet his gaze, his eyes searching mine.

"That thing. I hated not being able to say anything." I shook my head, not able to fully put into words how wretched it had made me feel. "I wanted you to kiss me, and to kiss you back, and not having your lips on mine … I just felt so … disconnected."

We sat for some time on the garage floor, until I shivered with cold. We went back into the house, and I went upstairs to run a bath, while Adam cleaned up in the garage. He came upstairs some minutes later with two mugs of tea and set mine on the side of the bath, before sitting on the closed lid of the toilet to drink his.

"Talk to me, Zoe." he said softly.

"I'm sorry" I whispered. "For forgetting my collar. It won't happen again, Sir."

"Good." He took a swallow of the tea. "How are your arms and shoulders?"

"Stiff." I raised my arms up over my head, circling my wrists, and winced in pain. "I'll live."

After dinner of steak and chips, we cuddled on the sofa listening to music. Adam was reading a book on the fall of the Roman Empire, while I tried to write in my journal. I still felt wretched about forgetting my collar, made worse by Adam's punishment. At first, I'd thought he was going to deny me my orgasm, but far worse than that had been the inability to hold and touch him – that most basic of human desire for physical contact - and to be denied the intimacy of kissing had been unbearable. I had clung to him afterwards and sobbed. Even now, I curled up on the sofa with my body pressed against his, desperate not to break that contact.

Later, when we went up to bed, I had lay on my side with Adam at my back, cradling me against his warm body. We had lay in silence, his hands holding mine, fingers laced together, and as I drifted off to sleep he whispered against the back of my neck.

"I love you sweetpea. You have no idea how much."

39

On Sunday I woke up to the smell of bacon, and padded downstairs to find him beating a pan of scrambled eggs. On the glass dining table there was a pot of coffee and two mugs, as well as orange juice and a plate of buttered toast.

"Sit" he turned to give me a quick peck before spooning the creamy egg mixture onto plates already laden with bacon, grilled tomatoes, mushrooms and baked beans. I poured the coffee into two mugs as he sat down, placing the food in front of me. "Do you want to do anything in particular today?"

"No, not really" I replied "I'm happy to do whatever you want, Sir"

He sighed, putting down his knife and fork. "Are you still cross with me for punishing you?"

It was my turn to sigh now, and I looked down at my plate as I spoke. "No not really. I mean I am, but I'm more cross at myself. I didn't mean to disobey your instruction. It was an oversight on my part, and it won't happen again." I looked up at met his gaze as I continued "Oh Adam, I hate this feeling that I've disappointed you."

"You could never disappoint me, sweetpea." He placed his hand on mine. "I was hurt and I over-reacted. You've had a lot on, what with the work situation, then with Angie turning up out of the blue to upset the routine. I should learn to be more tolerant and forgiving."

"And stop being quite such a control freak?" I asked, half smiling.

"That might just be a step too far, but we'll see." He smiled back, then lifted my hand to kiss my knuckles, before returning his attention back to the food. "So, shall we go for a walk? Maybe we could go over to Dimmingsdale again, and if you like I'll treat you to one of those massive wedges of cake afterwards in The Ramblers Retreat."

"Sounds good. Although I seem to recall the last time we went up there, ending up with my pants round my knees and a sore bum. Maybe we should stick to the main path around the lake this time."

"Spoil-sport" he laughed. "Come on then, eat up."

We went for a walk, then in the afternoon spent a little while making a final decision on the holiday accommodation we preferred, and picked the date so we could both put in our requests for annual leave. Sunday evening came far too quickly, and I said goodbye to Adam just after we had eaten.

"I'll call you tomorrow evening. Text me when you're home" I said, my arms around his neck as we kissed goodbye."

"Ok sweetpea. I hope the interviews go ok. I mean, I know you've decided not to employ Chris, and lord knows I can't stand the fella, but at least give him a chance and take it seriously – for his sake. Are you even going to let on that you and Ange go way back?"

"I didn't really want to, not yet anyway, but I suppose I'm going to have to tell him at some point. He'll figure it out soon enough – he's not stupid. I'll have to pick my moment, I guess."

"Ok, talk to you tomorrow. Night sexy."

40

I had scheduled the interview with Chris at 2pm on Monday, and booked the meeting room for the afternoon. I had managed to get half an hour with the MD, Mike, in the morning, and had broached the subject of getting new IT in place to better manage the telephone systems, and seemed open to the idea, although understandably he wanted to see some figures before he made any decisions, and suggested I put together some details of a couple of options. We agreed to get together in a fortnight, so that I could present a detailed proposal including costings. It was exactly the reaction I had hoped for, and would pave the way to getting a slightly higher salary, which I would need to do if I were to persuade Ange to take the job.

Chris came into the meeting room carrying wearing a new pink shirt and matching tie, and yet still smelling like damp dog. The dress code in the call centre had always been fairly informal. I didn't expect the guys to wear a shirt and tie as long as they were tidy, and not wearing denim or trainers, so he looked a little out of place. The shirt was obviously straight out of the packet, and he hadn't even bothered to iron it. It had the tell-tale fold lines down the front, but somehow he still managed to give off his ubiquitous fusty whiff, a bit like washing that hadn't been allowed to dry out properly. He carried a black leatherette document holder, and had insisted on providing the certificates for his educational qualifications, and also his "degree" which turned out to be a Diploma of Higher Education in Business Management. He spent half the allotted interview time telling me how fantastic the course had been and how it had given him skills that he felt he could use to benefit the company, and improve performance in the call centre, and yet he didn't seem able to answer any of my questions on how exactly he planned to do those things. He waffled his way round and about every question which I put to him, spouting bullshit and using his favourite jargon in an attempt to give the impression that he knew what he was talking about, and after 45 minutes, I was losing the will to live.

"Well, thanks for your time, Chris. I appreciate your enthusiasm and will certainly keep in mind some of your suggestions. Is there anything you'd like to ask?" Inside I was praying, please no, just get this over with.

"Just the obvious really. What will the new salary be, and what job title did you decide on? Obviously there needs to be a clearly defined hierarchy that the other staff understand, because most of them know me, and might think I'm being deliberately arrogant, rather than respecting the fact that I'm now their senior."

"Actually, I haven't made up my mind - on either. It will very much depend on the skills and attributes of the person appointed. I don't want to pigeon-hole the successful candidate by making them fit a rigid job spec." I replied, rising from my seat.

"Oh, I didn't realise you had any other applicants." It was meant as a question, and I addressed it as such.

"Yes, I have one more candidate to see this afternoon, but I'm certainly not going to rush the decision. It's more important that we hire the right individual, with not only the ambition, but also with the necessary skills and experience to implement the changes that we want to introduce. I need someone who will be able to make my life easier, but that could happen in any number of ways."

I ushered him out of the door before he could say any more, and poured myself a cup of coffee from the filter jug in the corner of the room. Angela would be here shortly, and I was hoping that Chris would be back at his desk with his headset on before she arrived. He was bound to be curious now, and I didn't want him to try and engage her in conversation if they met in the reception foyer.

Angela arrived bang on time. The interview had been a somewhat pointless exercise, given that I had known her for almost 20 years, so knew exactly what skill she had and what she could bring to the role. We chatted over coffee, about some of the options for new IT systems for call routing, the existing flow of call traffic and trends, and the reporting we had currently compared to the analytics I wanted in place, and the sort of systems she had used and trained on in the past. I also wanted to add the ability for web chat and online payments.

Afterwards we went downstairs and walked through the call centre so that Ange could get a look at the way we were currently running, with Chris watching our every move, needless to say. The team was much smaller than she had previously worked with, but she was already talking about changes she'd like to implement, all of which sounded really positive. By the time I showed her back to the foyer, I was both excited, and also nervous that I'd be able to secure a high enough salary for her to accept the job.

"Hiya!" I called as I arrived home, dropping my bag and kicking off my shoes off in the hallway. "So what did you think – really?"

"Well, your systems are antiquated, you definitely need a separate Customer Service team – you're expecting everyone to do too many different jobs to be good at any of them, and I hate those bloody wall boards – they've got to go!" She didn't pull any punches. "That said, you know I like a challenge, and something to get my teeth into would stop be feeling sorry for myself and constantly thinking about Mark and his new bit of fluff."

"So, you are considering it then? You'd actually stay?" I was thrilled.

"Well, it depends. I hate to be so materialistic Zoe, but I'd have to ask for more money than you're currently offering." I do want to be able to buy a place of my own, whether that's here, or somewhere else in the future. I don't know how you manage on what you earn."

"I know, I'll work on that, promise. If you took the job it would be a complete different scenario than just getting a supervisor to work with what we already have. I've already broached the subject with Mike, and he seems open to implementing some changes, so I'm going to meet with him again, and put forward some proposals next week, and I'll be sure to sing your praises. Leave it with me." With that, I went upstairs to get changed.

On Wednesday, Chris was hovering when I decided to nip out for a sandwich. I tried to ignore him, but as I stepped out of the door of the building, he announced that he was just going to buy some lunch too, so he'd walk with me.

"So, how did your other interview go? I thought you'd have made up your mind by now." He was certainly not beating about the bush.

"I don't think that's something I should be discussing with you Chris. Especially given that I'm on my lunch break. I'd like to leave work behind for half an hour, if you don't mind."

"Oh yeah, sorry. I was just hoping you'd made the right decision, even if it's not official yet." Then he stopped, his hand on my arm. "You know it makes sense to give me the job, don't you? I mean it could get a bit awkward if you don't."

I looked down at his hand on my sleeve, then looked back at him. "Chris, I don't know what you hope to achieve, but harassing me won't do you any favours." I was trying to be civil, rather than make a scene outside the coffee shop, but felt suddenly intimidated and snatched my arm away, before stepping inside to order my sandwich. When I came back out, he had disappeared, thank goodness.

When I returned to work with my sandwich and crisps, I found Chris already sat back at his desk, mid-call. I decided to go and approach Mike straight away, to see if I could get some more money on the table and entice Angela to take the job.

On Thursday morning I sent an email to Ange, formally offering her the position. I'd managed to convince Mike that she was the right person for the job, and sold him on the idea that she should come in as a Contact Centre Manager, shifting my role sideways to Customer Service Manager, so that we would work together at the same level. I had expected a decent increase to my own salary from April, but we agreed that I would defer that for now, on the basis that I offered her a fixed term contract for 12 months, with the go-ahead to implement the new technology that we so desperately needed. Then my pay review would take place in October, by which time we should have improved performance and sales.

That evening, Ange and I shared a bottle of wine, and we talked over the contract that was on the table.

"Look, I know it's still not quite what you're used to earning, but it's the best I can do."

"Babe, it's still 5k a year less than my last job. And that's without the private healthcare or gym membership, or free canteen" she frowned, topping up her glass."

"I know, but you'd be hard pushed to get that anywhere up here." I affected my best northern accent. "It's grim up North, you know. There's none of your fancy-shmansy bistros and sushi bars after work. If you live off chips and gravy like the rest of us, you'll save yourself a fortune, and put on a bit of fat to keep yourself warm through a northern winter! But seriously, you can stay here, pay half the bills and a bit towards my mortgage and we'd both be winning. You could still be putting some away each month towards a deposit on somewhere of your own. And what's 12 months? Call it a stopgap, while you settle things with Mark, and until you decide what or where you want to go next. And if you decide at the end of it that this area isn't for you, I won't try and persuade you to stay. Please at least say you'll sleep on it?"

Ange frowned, obviously deep in thought for a few moments, then spoke. "Zoe, you're the most infuriatingly sensible person I know. Ah fuck it - you just got yourself a new Manager and housemate. Cheers!"

"Yay!" we clinked our wine glasses together. "Cheers, lovely. You won't regret it."

I phoned Adam to tell him the good news, although he didn't seem in the least surprise.

"Makes perfect sense to me" he said, "You get the perfect person for the job, and she gets a fresh start and something to take her mind off Mr Man-bun. I wonder how Chris is going to react?"

"Probably not well. I'll tell him tomorrow afternoon. That way he won't have the chance to react and will have the weekend to get over it and calm down."

"Or just stew, and get worked up about it?" Adam replied. "Never mind, the prick didn't deserve the job, plain and simple. You'd end up carrying him and be no better off this time next year. In fact, from what you've said, you'd probably end up just losing staff."

"Probably. Anyway, we should celebrate. Why don't we go out somewhere for tea, Ange too, then I'll come back to yours afterwards?"

"Ok, sounds good. I'll book somewhere" he agreed. "I tell you what, I'll get off early, pick up Ange, then we can meet you at work. I'll book that Italian in town if you like. Is Ange insured to drive your car back afterwards, if we go straight to mine? Or you could leave it there until Sunday and I'll drop you off to pick it up on your way home?"

"Yeah, I suppose so. Do me a favour though, don't come into the car park." I asked.

"What, worried I'll embarrass you again? I've learnt that lesson, don't worry."

"No, it's not that" I replied, "I just don't want Chris to see that Ange in the car with you and recognise her. That way he's sure to know we're already friends, and I don't want him reading anything into it or accusing me of favouritism."

"Hmm, you're right, it would be rubbing his nose in it. On second thoughts…"

"No! Don't be cruel." I laughed. "He's an idiot, but he's harmless, and he's still my top call-taker. I need to keep him on side. Besides, Ange will be able to whip him into shape."

"Ok sweetpea, see you about quarter past. I'll park on the other side of the road, and wear my balaclava, and I'll lend Ange some sunglasses and a fake moustache if you like."

"Yeah, you would as well. Make it closer to half past, and just text we when you're outside."

"Ok sexy, see you tomorrow. Love you."

"Love you too."

42

The following day, I asked Chris to pop upstairs to the meeting room at 4:45. I could have just sent an email telling him he hadn't got the job, but that seemed a bit mean, so I typed up a very nice rejection letter to give to him as a formality after I'd spoken to him.

"Hi Chris, I wanted to have a chat to thank you for your application, but to tell you personally that you haven't been successful. We decided to go with the candidate who had far more management experience, but also more knowledge of IT and can help with implementing the new software that we want to install. I hope you'll take it on the chin, and continue to work as hard as you do, supporting both myself and the new Call Centre Manager."

"What? Call Centre Manager? And you never mentioned wanting to install new software." He was obviously livid. "That's bullshit Zoe, I could learn that stuff, just like anyone else can. You said you wanted a Supervisor, someone to just manage the calls and sort out the rotas and shit."

"Look, initially that's what I thought we needed, but the lady that's coming in has far more experience and skills in other areas too, so Mike has decided to take advantage of that. She'll only be here on a 12 month contract, so there may well be a chance to set up again after that, or other opportunities may come along in the meantime which may better suit you." He snatched the envelope from my outstretched hand and stormed back downstairs. It was almost time to turn the phones off, so I followed him a few minutes later, hoping he had just logged off and left.

Sure enough, Chris was nowhere to be seen when I went back in. I turned the lines over to the out of hours messaging service, and people started shutting down their PCs and wandering off, chatting about their plans for the weekend.

"Night ladies," I called to a couple of girls that waved as they went. "See you Monday. Have a good one. Night Dave, enjoy your weekend." As the call centre emptied, I checked my emails, flagging those that needed looking at first thing on Monday, and forwarding a couple of others to different team members to deal with.

"Don't stay too late" Mike was heading off too and raised his hand as he walked by. "It'll all still be there on Monday morning."

"I know, I won't be long." I smiled at him, "See you Monday."

Fifteen minutes later my phone buzzed. It was Ange, to say they were waiting across the street. I shut down my computer and grabbed my bag, then turned off the lights as I made my way to the front door. Finally, I set the alarm and locked up.

43

When I turned towards my car, my heart sank. Chris's was parked next to mine, and he stood leaning against his door, waiting for me. Everyone else had gone, and it was getting dark, but for the lights above the main doorway.

"I thought you'd left already." I tried to sound up-beat. "Not out on the town tonight?"

"I wanted a word" he said, flatly. "I thought I'd give you the chance to change your mind."

"Chris, I'm really sorry, but that's not going to happen."

"I think you'll be the one who's sorry" he leered, taking out his phone. "Unless you want the whole world to know about your kinky lovelife, that is."

I was stunned "What the hell...?" He was scrolling through his phone, then found what he was looking for, and held it up to my face.

"I was getting a takeaway last weekend and you drove past me in your car, so I followed you to see if you wanted to get a drink and talk about the job. Only you weren't going home, were you." He paused, as I watched the jerky video that was playing in front of me. It had been filmed through the blinds at Adams house. The colour must have drained from my face as I watched myself kneel, then stand again as Adam fastened the heavy collar around my neck.

"Oh, this is the good bit." he chuckled, as the video showed my struggling to take off my jeans. "Do people know what kind of guy you're dating? Nice arse, by the way. I said you'd be a handful."

With that he stepped forward and pressed himself against me, his hand on my neck as he tried to kiss me. I turned my face away, grabbing at the phone, while at the same time, bringing my knee up sharply to connect with his balls.

"Oomph! You fucking bitch!" Suddenly he grabbed my arm and spun me round so I had my front pressed against the car, my arm up my back. His hand was over my mouth, and with my free hand I pulled at his fingers trying to get free. His knee was between my legs. "I bet you like it rough. Is that where I went wrong?" His other hand was tugging at my skirt, and I was trying to scream but his hand was over my mouth and nose.

Then everything happened in a blur. I heard footsteps running, then an almighty roar, and as Chris was yanked away, pulling me with him, I fell to the ground. I landed badly on my knee and cried out in pain, then I looked around to see Adam grab Chris by his collar and pull him to his feet. He threw a right hook that connected with Chris's jaw and sent him reeling into the wall of the building, where he slid to the floor. Adam went to grab him again.

"Stop! You'll kill him!" I screamed, and almost as if he'd forgotten I was there, Adam spun around to face me. He looked down at my torn tights and bloody knee, and dropped down to crouch at my side.

"Shit, baby, are you ok? Where are you hurt?" He pushed my hair away from my face, now streaked with tears and mascara. "Shh, it's ok – it's over." He helped me get to my feet.

"It will be when I call the police – you could've broken my jaw, you sick fucker!" Chris picked up his phone with one hand, while massaging his jaw with the other.

"Like hell you will!" Adam knocked the phone from his hand, and Ange picked it up from the floor where it had landed at her feet.

"Zoe, what the hell happened? Are you ok hun?" she wrapped a protective arm around me, then turned on Adam. "I know you said to wait in the car, but will someone tell me what the fuck's going on here?"

"Hah, your new boss likes to play rough, that's what." Chris spoke as he stood up, "Her and this

neanderthal starred in their very own porn video."
Adam went to grab him again, but Chris anticipated
it, and ducked around the front of the car. "Hey,
listen fella, I did try to warn your whore girlfriend
that it would get really awkward if she didn't give me
the job, but she just wouldn't take the hint."

"What? All this is about the job? Wait, what video?"
Ange couldn't believe what she was hearing.

"He filmed us on his phone, through the front
window." I looked at Adam began crying again. "Last
weekend, when you were cross at me."

"What the hell did you do to her?" Ange yelled at
Adam, standing toe to toe, in total disregard of her
tiny frame against his six foot four bulk.

"Whoa, I'm not the bad guy in all this." He stepped
backwards, holding his hands up in a gesture of
surrender. "We were just playing. Surely you know
I'd never cause her any harm."

"I'm calling the police" Ange said, taking her own
phone out of her pocket.

"No don't – please!" I cried out. "I just want to go
home." I sighed and bent down to pick up my bag
and its contents from the tarmac, pressing the
remote on my keys to unlock the car door.

"Well, you can't drive." Ange took the keys from my hand, then looked at the cracked iphone she was holding.

"Hey, give that back!" Chris shouted.

"Or what?" Adam took it from her and put it in his jacket pocket.

"I could have you arrested for theft, as well as assault!" Chris stammered, stepping forward, but Adam turned on him. His face was just inches from the other man when he spoke.

"Listen to me, you sniveling little ginger bastard. You've got two witnesses here that would gladly see you put away for attempted rape as well as ABH. And shall we throw in stalking and filming someone in their own home without consent, while we're at it? I'm sure the police would have a field day. I'd call it using reasonable force to stop you from assaulting my girlfriend, but if you don't agree, then you go ahead and call the police. Here, pal, use my phone."

Adam continued to glare, his phone in his outstretched hand, until Chris backed off, stammering about it all being a misunderstanding, and how things had "got a bit out of hand." He got into his car, and was about to pull the door shut, when Adam stopped him. He leaned into the car, and planting a firm hand on Chris's shoulder, whispered something that neither of us heard, before standing back to let him drive off, tyres screeching.

Afterwards he pulled me into his arms, and we stood for several minutes, my arms wrapped tightly around his back, and my face buried into his neck while he stroked my hair.

"What did you say to him?" I asked as I pulled away.

"I just told him what I'd do to him if I ever found him anywhere near you or this place ever again. Oh, and not to bother contacting you for a reference." He gave my hand a squeeze. "Now, are you sure you're ok? Do you want to go and get checked out?"

"No, it's just a graze" I looked down at my knee, which had at least stopped bleeding. "It doesn't half sting though."

"OK, let's get you home." He turned to Ange, "Can you take Zoe's car back? I'll take care of her."

"Wait just a minute, I want to know what you did to her." She turned to me, "Zoe, you don't have to go with him. I'll take you home. I want to make sure you're *really* ok."

"Please Ange, I just want to spend the weekend with Adam." She looked at me in disbelief. "It's ok, really. I know you're worried about me, but there's no need to." I put my arms around my friend and hugged her tightly. "I'll call you in the morning, just so you know I'm ok. Stop worrying."

"I don't know – this doesn't feel right. Why did he get angry, and what did he do to you, hun?"

"Listen, you know when we were in Bath, and you made a silly remark about Adam spanking me?" I was glad it was dark so she couldn't see me blushing bright red. "I did something naughty … and he was … punishing me, if you know what I mean. It was nothing to worry about."

"Oh my god, and that pervert videoed you?" She turned to Adam. "Jesus, no wonder you punched him. Listen, I'm sorry if I got the wrong end of the stick."

"Don't worry about it. You were looking out for your friend. I'm grateful she's got you in her corner." He put his arm around my shoulder, and once again the gesture made me feel protected and totally safe. "Listen, shall we go out for Sunday lunch, if you're up to it? We were supposed to be celebrating, remember?"

"That sounds good." I replied, looking to Ange "Please, lets just forget tonight ever happened and move on. What do you reckon to a nice country pub lunch?"

"OK, but none of your northern 'chips and gravy' shite. I'm used to sushi bars and posh bistros, remember?"

I laughed, and Adam looked a little bemused. "I'll explain later, babe, but right now I could murder chips and gravy, and maybe a pie too. I'm bloody starving!"

"Ok, come on. Have you got everything?"

"Oh wait, I just need something from my car." I went round to the passenger side door and leaned in to take the small black box from inside the glove compartment, just as Ange started the engine. "Thanks babe, see you Sunday. I'll give you a ring to let you know what time we'll pick you up."

"All set now?" Adam asked, as we crossed over the street to where he had left is car.

"Yes Sir. I won't forget this again in a hurry." I took the necklace from its box and fastened if around my neck.

He said, kissed the back of my hand before placing it on his thigh and covering it with his own. "That's my good girl."

* * * * * * *

Printed in Great Britain
by Amazon

19494566R00139